Doctor Who Meets the Replicators and SG-1

Doctor Who Meets the Replicators and SG-1

The Ultimate Battle for Survival

Matthew Petchinsky

Apophis Enterprises LLC

Doctor Who Meets the Replicators and SG-1: The Ultimate Battle for Survival

By: Matthew Petchinsky

| 2 |

Disclaimer

This book is a fan-made creation and is intended solely for entertainment purposes. It is not an official product and has no affiliation with or endorsement from the creators, producers, or copyright holders of Doctor Who, Stargate SG-1, or any related properties. All characters, locations, and trademarks mentioned within this book are the property of their respective owners. This work does not intend to infringe upon the original copyrights and trademarks. The author acknowledges and respects the rights of the original creators and encourages readers to support the official releases.

Chapter 1: The Arrival of the Doctor

The TARDIS materialized with its familiar wheezing groan, blue light flickering against the dimly lit walls of Cheyenne Mountain. As the sound faded, an eerie silence followed, quickly shattered by blaring sirens and the hurried footsteps of military personnel. Sarah Jane Smith, her brow furrowed with concern, glanced at the Doctor.

"Where are we this time, Doctor?" she asked, adjusting her grip on her bag.

The Doctor, his eyes sparkling with curiosity, stepped out of the TARDIS and surveyed their surroundings. "Ah, Sarah Jane, it appears we've landed in some sort of military installation. Quite fascinating, really."

Before he could elaborate, they were surrounded by armed guards, weapons aimed and faces stern. Red lights flashed in the background, casting an ominous glow over the scene. The Doctor raised his hands in a gesture of peace, his expression one of mild amusement.

"Now, now, no need for all this fuss. I'm the Doctor, and this is Sarah Jane Smith," he said, his voice calm and reassuring.

A burly man in uniform, his face lined with authority, stepped forward. "I'm General George Hammond. You and your... machine just appeared out of nowhere. You're on highly classified grounds. Identify yourselves properly."

The Doctor gave a charming smile. "As I said, I'm the Doctor. Just the Doctor. And Sarah Jane here is my companion. We're travelers, you might say."

Hammond's eyes narrowed. "Travelers? From where exactly?"

The Doctor opened his mouth to respond, but Sarah Jane interjected. "It's a bit complicated, General. We're not from around here, let's put it that way."

Before Hammond could press further, a group of people in military attire arrived, clearly the core team. The leader, a tall man with an air of authority, spoke first. "I'm Colonel Jack O'Neill, this is Major Samantha Carter, Dr. Daniel Jackson, and Teal'c."

The Doctor nodded to each in turn. "Pleasure to meet you all. Now, can someone tell me what this place is?"

Carter stepped forward, her scientific curiosity piqued. "This is the SGC, the Stargate Command. We deal with threats from other planets through the Stargate."

The Doctor's face lit up with interest. "Stargate, you say? I've never encountered such a thing. What exactly is it?"

Hammond sighed, motioning for the guards to lower their weapons. "The Stargate is an ancient device that allows for instant travel between distant planets. We use it to explore and defend Earth from various alien threats."

"Intriguing," the Doctor mused, rubbing his chin. "And what sort of threats do you face?"

O'Neill crossed his arms. "Our current problem is something called the Replicators. They're advanced, self-replicating machines that consume everything in their path. Very dangerous."

The Doctor's eyes widened slightly. "Replicators, you say? Never heard of them. Sounds like a serious threat. What can you tell me about them?"

Carter stepped in. "They're composed of nanotechnology and are highly adaptive. We've had some success fighting them, but it's a constant battle. Your timing is... interesting, to say the least."

Sarah Jane looked around at the tense faces. "Doctor, do you think we can help?"

The Doctor nodded thoughtfully. "I believe so, Sarah Jane. But first, I need to understand more about these Replicators. Colonel O'Neill, General Hammond, if you would be so kind as to brief me further."

Hammond exchanged a look with O'Neill and nodded. "Alright, Doctor. Follow us. We'll take you to the briefing room and bring you up to speed."

As they walked through the corridors of the SGC, the Doctor's mind raced with possibilities. This was a new challenge, a new mystery to unravel. And with the help of SG-1, he was determined to find a way to stop the Replicators and save Earth once more.

Chapter 2: Discovery of the Replicators

The briefing room was a hive of activity as General Hammond and SG-1 explained the intricacies of the Replicators to the Doctor and Sarah Jane. Maps and images displayed on the large screen showed the devastating capabilities of these mechanical invaders.

"As you can see," Hammond said, pointing to an image of a Replicator block, "these machines are highly advanced and capable of rapid self-replication. They've devastated entire worlds, consuming all available resources to build more of themselves."

The Doctor leaned forward, his expression one of intense concentration. "So, they're essentially a form of mechanical life, driven by an insatiable need to reproduce and evolve. What measures have you taken to combat them?"

Colonel Jack O'Neill, arms crossed and face set in a grim line, spoke up. "We've tried everything from heavy artillery to advanced alien technology. They adapt too quickly. Every time we think we have an edge, they change the game."

Major Samantha Carter, standing beside the screen, nodded. "Their adaptability is their greatest strength. We're constantly trying to find new ways to counter them, but it's a constant battle."

Sarah Jane, sitting beside the Doctor, asked, "And what about their weaknesses? There must be something we can exploit."

Dr. Daniel Jackson, adjusting his glasses, responded, "We've had some success with certain energy weapons, but it's always temporary. The Replicators learn and adapt."

Meanwhile, in London, a Replicator ship entered in the city through a rift that is within the city of London and through a rift within Cardiff. They wasted no time in beginning their invasion to feed and assimilate and replicate themselves.

Suddenly, the intercom crackled to life, and Walter Harriman's voice came through with urgency. "General Hammond, we have an emergency situation. Reports are coming in of Replicator activity in London and Cardiff."

The room fell silent for a moment as the gravity of the situation sank in. Hammond immediately snapped into action. "Get me a secure line to UNIT and Torchwood. We need to coordinate our response."

The Doctor stood abruptly, his face a mask of concern. "London? Cardiff? We need to act quickly. The Replicators won't waste any time. They'll consume everything in their path."

Carter was already at her console, typing furiously. "Establishing a secure link now, General."

The screen flickered, and the familiar face of Kate Stewart, head of UNIT, appeared, looking stressed and urgent. "This is Kate Stewart of UNIT. London is under attack by an unknown mechanical force. They're spreading rapidly, and our defenses are being overwhelmed. We need assistance immediately!"

The feed split to show Captain Jack Harkness at Torchwood's Hub in Cardiff, his usual confident demeanor replaced by a look of deep concern. "Doctor, if you're there, we need help. These things are tearing through our defenses like they're nothing. What are we dealing with?"

The Doctor stepped forward, his tone decisive. "Those are Replicators, Jack. Highly advanced, self-replicating machines. General Hammond, we need to establish continuous communication with UNIT and Torchwood. They need all the support we can offer."

Hammond nodded. "Major Carter, make it happen. Colonel O'Neill, prepare a team for possible deployment. We need to be ready for anything."

Carter's fingers flew over the keyboard. "Establishing continuous secure link now."

The Doctor turned to Kate Stewart and Jack Harkness on the screen. "Kate, Jack, this is the Doctor. I'm at the SGC with SG-1. We're coordinating a response. Give me your current status."

Kate Stewart responded first, her voice tense. "London is being overrun. The Replicators are spreading through the city, consuming everything. We've evacuated as many civilians as possible, but it's chaos. We need immediate assistance."

Jack Harkness added, "Cardiff is holding for now, but it's only a matter of time before they break through. We need a plan, Doctor."

The Doctor nodded. "Alright. Major Carter, do you have any detailed scans of the Replicators' activity?"

Carter pulled up a map on the screen, showing hotspots of Replicator activity. "Doctor, we've detected high levels of activity in London and Cardiff. They're expanding rapidly and consuming everything."

The Doctor studied the map, his mind racing. "We need to disrupt their network. If we can introduce a virus or some sort of feedback loop, we might be able to slow them down."

Daniel Jackson interjected, "Do you have experience with creating such a virus, Doctor?"

The Doctor smiled slightly. "I've had my moments. But I'll need access to your technology and some time to work out the details."

O'Neill clapped his hands together. "Alright, Carter, give the Doctor whatever he needs. Teal'c, Daniel, you're with me. We'll prep for a ground operation in case things go south."

Hammond addressed the room. "We have a lot of lives at stake. Let's get to work. Doctor, you have our full support."

The room buzzed with activity as everyone sprang into action. The Doctor turned to Sarah Jane, his expression determined. "Looks like we're in for a bit of a fight, Sarah."

She smiled bravely. "Wouldn't have it any other way, Doctor."

With the link established and plans in motion, the Doctor knew they had a chance to stop the Replicators. But the clock was ticking, and failure was not an option. He turned back to the screen, where Kate and Jack were waiting for further instructions.

"Kate, Jack, we need to set up a coordinated defense. Major Carter will be sending you data on the Replicators' weak points. Focus your efforts on those areas. We'll work on developing a virus to disrupt their network."

Kate Stewart nodded, her face resolute. "Understood, Doctor. We'll hold the line as best we can."

Jack Harkness gave a grim smile. "You can count on us, Doctor. Just hurry. We're running out of time."

As the communication ended, the Doctor turned to Major Carter. "Major, let's get to work on that virus. We need to move fast."

Carter nodded, already bringing up schematics and data on her console. "Right. Let's see what we can come up with."

The Doctor and Carter dove into the data, their minds working in tandem as they devised a plan to stop the Replicators. Time was of the essence, and the fate of London—and possibly the world—hung in the balance.

Chapter 3: Torchwood's Encounter

The Torchwood Hub buzzed with its usual chaotic energy. Amidst the alien artifacts and high-tech equipment, Captain Jack Harkness and his team were gathered around a console, studying a strange signal that had appeared on their radar. Jack's immortal eyes scanned the data, but even with his vast knowledge, he couldn't make sense of it.

"Alright, team," Jack said, his voice cutting through the hum of machines, "we've got something strange on our hands. Gwen, what have we got?"

Gwen Cooper, Torchwood's resident investigator, looked up from her screen. "It's a signal, alright. But it's not like anything we've seen before. It's repeating at regular intervals, almost like a beacon."

Ianto Jones, ever the meticulous archivist, added, "It's not coming from any known source. I've cross-referenced it with everything in our database. It's completely alien."

Jack frowned, his mind racing. "Alien, but not anything we've encountered. Alright, team, we're heading out. I want to know what we're dealing with. Tosh, keep monitoring the signal and guide us to the source."

As they geared up, Jack's mind lingered on the conversation with the Doctor. Replicators, the Doctor had called them. Machines that consumed everything in their path. But Jack had never encountered them, despite his centuries of life. That worried him more than anything.

They piled into the SUV, and Jack floored the accelerator. The streets of Cardiff flashed by as they followed Toshiko Sato's directions, her voice calm and precise over the comms.

"Turn left here," Tosh instructed. "The signal is getting stronger. It's coming from the industrial district."

They pulled up outside an old, abandoned factory. The air was thick with tension as they exited the vehicle. Jack led the way, his eyes scanning their surroundings. The signal was definitely stronger here. Gwen, Ianto, and Owen Harper flanked him, weapons at the ready.

They moved silently through the dilapidated building, their footsteps echoing off the walls. Suddenly, Gwen held up a hand. "Listen," she whispered.

A faint, mechanical clattering sound reached their ears, growing louder as they advanced. Jack's heart raced. This was it. Whatever was causing the signal was just ahead.

They turned a corner and came face to face with a swarm of Replicators. The mechanical creatures skittered across the floor, climbing walls and machinery with frightening speed. For a moment, the team was frozen in shock.

"What the hell are those?" Owen exclaimed, raising his weapon.

"Replicators," Jack said grimly, recalling the Doctor's description. "Nasty pieces of work. We need to contain them, now!"

The team opened fire, bullets sparking off the metallic bodies of the Replicators. But for every one they destroyed, more seemed to take its place. The machines adapted quickly, shifting and reforming, their relentless advance unstoppable.

"Tosh, we need backup!" Jack shouted into his comms. "There are too many of them!"

Tosh's voice came back, strained with urgency. "I'm trying to contact UNIT, but the Replicators are interfering with communications. Hold on!"

Gwen aimed her weapon, taking out several Replicators, but it was a losing battle. "Jack, we can't keep this up! We need a plan!"

Jack's mind raced. "Fall back! We need to regroup and figure out a new strategy. Tosh, any ideas?"

Tosh's voice crackled through the static. "There's a power junction nearby. If we can lure them there, we might be able to overload the system and fry their circuits."

Jack nodded. "Alright, you heard her. Fall back to the junction. Go, go, go!"

The team retreated, firing as they went, trying to keep the Replicators at bay. They reached the junction, and Jack quickly assessed the situation. "Ianto, get those wires exposed. Gwen, Owen, cover him!"

Ianto worked swiftly, his hands steady despite the chaos. Sparks flew as he pulled the wires free. "Ready!"

Jack grabbed the wires, his eyes meeting Gwen's. "When I say now, hit the switch. Everyone else, keep those things off us!"

The Replicators were closing in, their mechanical legs clattering on the concrete floor. Jack held the wires, waiting for the right moment. "Now, Gwen!"

Gwen slammed the switch, and Jack thrust the wires into the swarm of Replicators. Electricity surged through the machines, causing them to convulse and spark. One by one, they fell, their circuits overloaded.

The team watched in awe as the Replicators collapsed, the air filled with the smell of burnt metal. Jack let out a breath he didn't realize he'd been holding. "That was too close."

Gwen wiped sweat from her brow. "Jack, we can't handle this alone. We need more help."

Jack nodded. "You're right. Tosh, get me the Doctor. We need to figure out how to stop these things for good."

Back at the Hub, Tosh managed to establish a shaky connection to the SGC. The Doctor's face appeared on the screen, his expression serious. "Jack, what's your status?"

"We had a run-in with the Replicators," Jack replied. "We managed to fry a bunch of them, but they're adapting too fast. We need more firepower and a better plan."

The Doctor nodded. "Understood. We're working on a solution here. Stay strong, Jack. Help is on the way."

As the connection ended, Jack turned to his team. "Alright, people. This is far from over. But we're Torchwood, and we don't back down. Let's get ready for the next round."

With the Replicators temporarily disabled, the team knew it was only a matter of time before they faced the next wave. But with the Doctor's help and their unwavering determination, they were ready to fight.

Chapter 4: UNIT Mobilizes

The morning sun cast long shadows over the streets of London as UNIT Headquarters buzzed with activity. The atmosphere was tense, as reports of the Replicator invasion had reached them just hours ago. Inside the command center, the urgency was palpable.

Kate Stewart stood at the helm, her expression a mask of calm determination. "Status update," she called out, her voice cutting through the controlled chaos.

A young officer, Lieutenant Adams, looked up from his console. "Ma'am, we've confirmed multiple points of entry. The Replicators have touched down in several locations across the city. Our forces are engaging, but they're spreading quickly."

Kate nodded, absorbing the information. "Alright. We need to contain this threat before it gets out of hand. What's the status on civilian evacuation?"

Captain Mike Yates, standing nearby, stepped forward. "Evacuations are underway, but it's slow going. The Replicators are causing widespread panic."

Kate's mind raced as she formulated a plan. "We need to divide our forces. Captain Yates, take a team and focus on evacuations. Lieutenant Adams, coordinate with local law enforcement and get them to assist in maintaining order. I'll lead the main assault team."

Adams nodded. "Yes, ma'am. I'll get right on it."

Yates gave a sharp salute. "Understood, Kate. We won't let you down."

As the officers dispersed to carry out their orders, Kate turned to her tactical advisor, Sergeant Benton. "Benton, what can you tell me about the Replicators? Any weaknesses we can exploit?"

Benton scratched his head, clearly frustrated. "Not much, I'm afraid. They're highly adaptive, and traditional weapons are only marginally effective. We need something more."

Kate sighed. "Then we need to think outside the box. Let's get the lab boys working on something unconventional. Maybe a new type of EMP or a frequency disruptor. In the meantime, we fight with what we've got."

A comms officer called out, "Ma'am, we have a priority message from the SGC. It's the Doctor."

Kate's eyes lit up with a glimmer of hope. "Patch him through."

The screen flickered, and the Doctor's face appeared, looking grave but determined. "Kate, how are you holding up?"

"We're managing, Doctor, but it's not looking good. The Replicators are everywhere, and we're struggling to contain them," Kate replied.

The Doctor nodded. "I've been working with SG-1 on a plan to disrupt their network. We're developing a virus that should slow them down. But we need more time."

Kate clenched her jaw. "Time is something we don't have much of, Doctor. But we'll hold the line. Just get that virus ready."

The Doctor's expression softened. "You're doing great, Kate. Hold tight, and we'll get through this."

The connection ended, and Kate turned to Benton. "Alright, Sergeant. Let's get those experimental weapons ready. We need to buy the Doctor as much time as we can."

Benton nodded and rushed off to the lab. Kate took a deep breath and addressed the remaining officers. "Listen up, everyone. We're facing an unprecedented threat. But we are UNIT, and we will not falter. Get to your posts and prepare for battle."

Outside, the streets of London were in turmoil. Civilians ran in all directions, trying to escape the advancing Replicators. UNIT soldiers moved with precision, guiding people to safety and setting up defensive positions.

Captain Yates led his team through the chaos, his voice steady and authoritative. "Keep moving! Head to the designated evacuation points. We've got you covered."

In another part of the city, Lieutenant Adams coordinated with local law enforcement. "Set up barricades here and here. We need to funnel the civilians towards our safe zones."

As the main assault team geared up, Kate joined them on the front lines. Her presence was a beacon of strength for her soldiers. "Remember, these things may be advanced, but they can be beaten. We hold this line. No matter what."

The Replicators swarmed towards them, a tide of relentless mechanical invaders. The soldiers opened fire, their weapons lighting up the street. The Replicators' bodies sparked and shattered, but more kept coming.

Benton's voice crackled over the comms. "Kate, we've got something. The lab boys think they can rig a portable EMP. It won't stop them, but it might slow them down."

Kate's heart lifted. "Get it here now, Sergeant. We need every advantage we can get."

Minutes later, Benton arrived with the device, a makeshift contraption that hummed with energy. "Here it is, ma'am. Just activate it and stand back."

Kate nodded, taking the device. "Good work, Benton. Let's see if this buys us some breathing room."

She activated the EMP, and a wave of energy pulsed outwards, causing the Replicators to convulse and collapse. The soldiers cheered as the immediate threat was neutralized, but Kate knew it was only a temporary reprieve.

"We've got a window," she said, rallying her troops. "Let's use it. Push them back and give the Doctor the time he needs."

With renewed determination, UNIT forces surged forward, their resolve unshakable. They fought with everything they had, knowing that the fate of London—and perhaps the world—rested on their shoulders.

As the battle raged on, Kate couldn't shake the feeling that they were just holding back the tide. But she knew that with the Doctor's help, they had a chance. And as long as they had that, they would keep fighting. UNIT had faced impossible odds before, and they would do so again. For Earth, for humanity, for survival.

The battle for London had begun, and UNIT was ready to give it everything they had.

Chapter 5: Rose's Return

The SGC was abuzz with activity. Alarms blared intermittently, signaling the ongoing struggle against the Replicators. In the midst of this chaos, the Doctor and Major Carter were hunched over a console, working on the virus that might be their last hope.

"Doctor, if we can integrate this feedback loop into the virus, it should disrupt their neural network long enough for us to mount a counter-attack," Carter suggested, pointing to a schematic on the screen.

The Doctor nodded, his mind racing with possibilities. "Brilliant, Major. We need to amplify the signal to ensure it penetrates their entire network. Any ideas?"

Carter was about to respond when the room suddenly grew cold. The air seemed to shimmer, and a golden light filled the room. Everyone froze, eyes wide with shock and curiosity.

The light coalesced into a familiar figure, and the Doctor's hearts skipped a beat. "Rose?" he whispered, barely daring to believe his eyes.

Rose Tyler stood before them, looking just as she had the last time he saw her. Her face was etched with worry, but her eyes sparkled with determination. "Doctor, we need to talk. Now."

Sarah Jane, who had been assisting Carter with the technical aspects of the virus, gasped. "Rose? How is this possible?"

Rose took a deep breath, her voice urgent. "I've come from the parallel universe. The walls between dimensions are weakening, and it's because of the Replicators. They're not just a threat here; they're consuming realities."

The Doctor's eyes widened. "The Replicators are breaching the barriers between universes? How did you get here?"

Rose nodded. "It wasn't easy. The Dimension Cannon, it's been upgraded. But that's not important right now. Doctor, we don't have much time. They're coming."

Carter, who had been listening intently, stepped forward. "Rose, what do you know about the Replicators? Anything that can help us?"

Rose looked at the screen displaying the schematic of the virus. "The Replicators in our universe are even more advanced. They've found a way to evolve beyond their current state, becoming almost indestructible. But they have a weakness."

The Doctor's eyes lit up with hope. "What is it, Rose?"

Rose pointed to the feedback loop on the screen. "You're on the right track. But you need to create a multi-phased disruptor. One that targets their core processing units and their ability to adapt. It's the only way to stop them."

Carter frowned, deep in thought. "A multi-phased disruptor? That's going to require a lot more power and a precise delivery mechanism."

The Doctor grinned. "Power we can manage. Precision, that's always been my specialty. Rose, you're a genius."

Rose smiled, but her eyes remained serious. "Doctor, there's more. The Replicators are being controlled by something, or someone. We don't know who, but they're coordinating the attacks across dimensions."

Sarah Jane's face paled. "Someone is controlling them? That makes this even more dangerous."

The Doctor nodded. "Indeed. We need to find out who or what is behind this and stop them. Rose, any clues?"

Rose shook her head. "Not yet. But we have a lead. There's a signal, similar to the one the Replicators are using, but it's different. It's almost like a command signal."

Carter's eyes lit up with understanding. "If we can trace that signal, we might be able to find the source and shut it down."

The Doctor clapped his hands together. "Right, then. Major Carter, let's integrate Rose's information into our virus. We need to create that multi-phased disruptor and trace the signal. Sarah Jane, get in touch with UNIT and Torchwood. They need to be ready for anything."

As everyone sprang into action, Rose pulled the Doctor aside. "Doctor, there's something else you need to know. If we don't stop this, the barriers between realities will collapse completely. Everything, everywhere, will be consumed."

The Doctor placed a reassuring hand on her shoulder. "We'll stop it, Rose. I promise you. Together, we can do anything."

Rose nodded, her eyes filled with a mix of hope and fear. "I believe in you, Doctor. Always have."

The Doctor turned back to the task at hand, his mind racing. With Rose's information and the combined efforts of the SGC, UNIT, and Torchwood, they had a chance. A slim one, but a chance nonetheless.

Hours passed as they worked tirelessly. The virus was nearing completion, and the signal trace was almost ready. The tension in the room was palpable.

Finally, Carter looked up from her console, a triumphant smile on her face. "Doctor, we've got it. The multi-phased disruptor is ready, and we've traced the signal. It's coming from an unknown source deep in the void between dimensions."

The Doctor's eyes gleamed with determination. "Then that's where we're going. Rose, Sarah Jane, Major Carter, let's save the universes."

As they prepared for the final showdown, the Doctor couldn't shake the feeling that this was just the beginning. The Replicators were a formidable enemy, but with Rose by his side and the strength of their allies, he knew they could overcome anything.

The fight for survival had begun, and the Doctor was ready to face whatever lay ahead.

Chapter 6: SG-1's Arrival

The shimmering blue event horizon of the Stargate illuminated the gate room at the SGC. General Hammond stood at the base of the ramp, watching intently as the wormhole stabilized. Moments later, the familiar figures of SG-1 emerged, weapons at the ready and expressions set with determination.

Colonel Jack O'Neill was the first to speak. "General, we've tracked the Replicators' movements. They're spreading faster than we anticipated."

Major Samantha Carter nodded, her face grim. "They've adapted their tactics. We picked up signs of coordinated attacks across multiple planets. They're definitely being controlled by an external source."

Dr. Daniel Jackson, adjusting his glasses, added, "We found traces of an unusual signal, one that seems to be giving the Replicators their orders. It matches the one Rose described."

Teal'c, ever stoic, simply stated, "The threat is greater than anticipated. We must act swiftly."

Hammond nodded, his face reflecting the gravity of the situation. "SG-1, we've got a lot to catch up on. The Doctor and his allies are already working on a solution. Follow me to the briefing room."

As they made their way through the bustling corridors, the tension was palpable. Soldiers and scientists alike were on high alert, their movements hurried and purposeful. When they entered the briefing room, the Doctor, Rose, Sarah Jane, and Major Carter were already deep in discussion.

The Doctor looked up, his eyes bright with a mix of excitement and worry. "Colonel O'Neill, Major Carter, Dr. Jackson, Teal'c. Glad to see you all. We've made some progress."

O'Neill raised an eyebrow. "Progress is good. What have you got?"

Major Carter gestured to the console, where schematics and data were displayed. "We've developed a multi-phased disruptor that targets the Replicators' core processing units and their ability to adapt. With Rose's help, we've integrated this into a virus that should slow them down significantly."

The Doctor added, "And we've traced the command signal to a source deep in the void between dimensions. We believe this is where the control is coming from."

Teal'c's eyes narrowed. "A formidable enemy indeed. What is our next move?"

The Doctor's face hardened with resolve. "We need to deploy the virus and disruptor on a large scale. At the same time, we have to locate and neutralize the source of the command signal. It's a two-pronged attack. If we can disrupt their coordination and slow their replication, we stand a chance."

O'Neill nodded. "Sounds like a plan. How do we get this virus out there?"

Carter pointed to a device on the table. "We've modified some of our transportable emitters to broadcast the virus. We can place these at strategic points across the affected areas. But we'll need to get close."

Daniel Jackson looked thoughtful. "And what about the source? How do we get there?"

Rose stepped forward. "The Dimension Cannon. It's how I got here. It can be used to reach the void where the signal is originating. But it's risky."

The Doctor nodded. "Risky, but necessary. We'll need a small team to go in and shut it down. SG-1, Rose, and myself. The rest of you will handle the deployment of the virus."

General Hammond's voice was steady. "You have my full support. Let's make this happen."

Preparations began immediately. Soldiers loaded the transportable emitters onto vehicles, ready to be deployed across London and other key locations. The atmosphere was electric with a mix of fear and determination.

The Doctor turned to SG-1. "We'll need to synchronize our efforts perfectly. Timing is crucial."

O'Neill grinned. "Timing's our specialty. Let's get this done."

As they geared up, Rose approached the Doctor, her eyes filled with a mixture of emotions. "Doctor, promise me we'll stop them. Promise me we'll save everyone."

The Doctor placed a reassuring hand on her shoulder. "I promise, Rose. We'll save them. Together."

With the final preparations complete, the teams moved out. The Doctor, Rose, and SG-1 headed to the Dimension Cannon, while Sarah Jane and Major Carter coordinated the deployment of the virus.

The Dimension Cannon, a sleek device with a powerful hum, was set up in a secure room. Rose took a deep breath as she activated it, the air shimmering with energy. "Ready, Doctor?"

The Doctor nodded. "Let's do this."

In a flash of light, they were transported to the void between dimensions. The space was disorienting, a swirling mass of colors and shapes that defied comprehension. But amidst the chaos, a single structure stood out – a massive control hub, pulsing with an eerie glow.

Teal'c's eyes scanned the area. "We must move quickly. The source is near."

They approached the control hub cautiously, weapons at the ready. As they neared, a swarm of Replicators emerged, blocking their path. O'Neill raised his weapon. "Here we go!"

A fierce battle ensued. The Replicators were relentless, but SG-1 and the Doctor fought with everything they had. Teal'c's staff weapon blazed, cutting through the mechanical swarm, while Carter and Jackson provided cover fire.

The Doctor and Rose pushed forward, determined to reach the control hub. "Almost there!" the Doctor shouted, his voice barely audible over the din of battle.

Finally, they reached the hub. The Doctor pulled out a sonic screwdriver, working furiously to disable the controls. "Rose, I need you to hold them off for a few more seconds!"

Rose nodded, her resolve unshakable. "You got it, Doctor!"

With a final surge of effort, the Doctor disabled the control hub. The Replicators faltered, their coordination disrupted. O'Neill, Carter, Jackson, and Teal'c finished off the remaining machines, their expressions triumphant.

"We did it!" Carter exclaimed, her eyes shining with relief.

The Doctor turned to Rose, a broad smile on his face. "We did it. The command signal is down. The Replicators should be much more manageable now."

Back on Earth, the deployment of the virus had gone smoothly. The Replicators across London and other affected areas began to falter and collapse, their systems overloaded by the multi-phased disruptor.

General Hammond's voice came through the comms. "Doctor, SG-1, the virus is working. The Replicators are being neutralized."

The Doctor sighed with relief. "Excellent work, everyone. We've done it."

As they prepared to return to Earth, the Doctor couldn't help but feel a sense of pride and gratitude. They had faced an impossible enemy and come out victorious. And with allies like SG-1, UNIT, and Torchwood, he knew they could handle whatever challenges lay ahead.

The battle was won, but the war was not over. The Doctor and his companions knew there would always be more threats, more dangers. But for now, they had saved the day. And that was enough.

As they stepped back through the Dimension Cannon, returning to the SGC, the Doctor turned to Rose, a twinkle in his eye. "Welcome back, Rose. We've got a lot more adventures ahead of us."

Rose smiled, her eyes shining with the promise of new adventures. "I wouldn't have it any other way, Doctor. Let's save the universe."

And with that, they stepped into the future, ready to face whatever came next.

Chapter 7: Initial Clash

The skies over London were darkened by storm clouds, mirroring the chaos unfolding in the streets below. The Replicators swarmed through the city, their mechanical forms relentless and unstoppable. Amidst the turmoil, UNIT, Torchwood, and SG-1 had gathered, ready to make their stand.

The Doctor, standing on a makeshift command platform with Kate Stewart and Colonel Jack O'Neill, surveyed the scene. "We need to disrupt their network and push them back. Sarah Jane, you and Captain Jack take the west side with Torchwood. Colonel O'Neill, Major Carter, Dr. Jackson, Teal'c, you're with me."

Kate Stewart nodded, her expression resolute. "UNIT will hold the line and assist where needed. We need to protect the civilians and prevent the Replicators from spreading."

As orders were given and teams mobilized, the Doctor turned to Sarah Jane, his eyes filled with determination. "Stay safe, Sarah Jane. We're going to need everyone to make it through this."

Sarah Jane smiled, her bravery shining through. "You too, Doctor. Let's save London."

With a final nod, the teams split up, each heading to their designated areas. The streets of London were eerily quiet, the only sounds the distant clattering of Replicator legs and the hum of approaching battle.

Captain Jack Harkness led Torchwood through the labyrinthine alleys of the west side. Gwen Cooper, Ianto Jones, and Owen Harper moved with precision, their weapons ready.

"We need to cut off their advance here," Jack said, pointing to a narrow street choked with debris. "Gwen, take the left flank. Ianto, cover the right. Owen, you're with me."

Gwen nodded, her expression fierce. "Got it, Jack. Let's show these things what Torchwood is made of."

As they took their positions, a swarm of Replicators rounded the corner, their metallic bodies glinting in the dim light. Gwen opened fire, her shots precise and lethal. Ianto's portable energy disruptor sent arcs of electricity through the machines, causing them to convulse and collapse.

Jack and Owen moved forward, cutting through the Replicators with a combination of bullets and close-quarter combat. The mechanical invaders fell, but more took their place, their numbers seemingly endless.

"Jack, we're being overrun!" Owen shouted, taking down a Replicator that had leapt at him.

Jack's jaw tightened. "We need reinforcements. Gwen, get on the comms and call for backup from UNIT."

Gwen ducked behind cover, her fingers flying over her communicator. "UNIT, this is Torchwood. We're under heavy attack on the west side. Requesting immediate backup."

A voice crackled through the comms. "This is UNIT, we're sending reinforcements now. Hold your position."

Jack fired another volley at the approaching swarm. "Just hold on, team. Help is on the way."

In the north sector, SG-1 advanced through the narrow streets, Major Carter leading the way with her scanner. "We need to find their central hub and upload the virus."

Teal'c's staff weapon blazed, cutting down Replicators as they advanced. "We are close, Major Carter. I can sense their energy signature."

Colonel O'Neill covered their flank, his P90 spraying bullets. "Then let's move. The sooner we get this done, the better."

Daniel Jackson, using his sidearm, kept pace with the team. "There, up ahead. That building looks like a command center."

They reached the building, but it was heavily guarded by Replicators. Carter set up an EMP device, her fingers moving quickly. "I need a minute to get this online."

O'Neill and Teal'c provided cover, their weapons keeping the Replicators at bay. Daniel joined Carter, helping her set up the device. "Almost there, Sam."

With a high-pitched whine, the EMP activated, sending out a pulse that caused the Replicators to convulse and collapse. The team moved into the building, determined to find the central hub.

Meanwhile, the Doctor and Sarah Jane moved between sectors, using their sonic devices to hack into the Replicators' networks. They encountered a small squad of UNIT soldiers pinned down by a relentless wave of Replicators.

"Doctor, over here!" Sarah Jane called out, pointing to the beleaguered UNIT team.

The Doctor nodded, his sonic screwdriver emitting a high-frequency pulse that caused the Replicators to momentarily pause. "Sarah Jane, help the soldiers regroup. I'll handle these tin cans."

Sarah Jane quickly moved to assist the UNIT team, providing cover and rallying them. The Doctor, with his usual flair, dodged and weaved through the Replicators, using his sonic screwdriver to disrupt their circuitry. "Come on, you metal monstrosities! Let's see how you handle a bit of Time Lord technology!"

The combined efforts of UNIT, Torchwood, and SG-1 were beginning to turn the tide. The Replicators, though numerous and adaptive, were struggling against the coordinated assault. The multi-phased disruptors and EMP devices were proving effective, but it was clear this was only a temporary solution.

Back at the command center, Kate Stewart monitored the battle through a series of screens. "All units, report in. How's it looking out there?"

Colonel O'Neill's voice came through the comms. "We're holding, but these things keep coming. We need to find their command center and shut it down for good."

Captain Jack Harkness chimed in next. "West sector is under control, but we've got heavy resistance. We're moving towards their control node now."

The Doctor's voice was the last to report. "We've managed to disrupt their communications here. Keep pressing forward, everyone. We're making progress."

Kate nodded, her resolve unwavering. "Keep it up. We're almost there."

As the battle raged on, the Doctor and Sarah Jane regrouped with SG-1 and Torchwood at a central junction. The area was littered with the remains of Replicators, but the path ahead was still swarming with active machines.

The Doctor addressed the group, his tone urgent. "We need to reach their command center and deploy the virus. It's our best chance to stop them."

Carter stepped forward, holding the device. "We've got the virus ready. We just need to get close enough to upload it."

Jack Harkness cracked his knuckles, a determined smile on his face. "Then let's not waste any more time."

The combined forces of UNIT, Torchwood, and SG-1 moved as one, pushing through the Replicator hordes with relentless determination. The Doctor led the way, his sonic screwdriver and quick thinking guiding them through the chaos.

Finally, they reached the heart of the Replicator infestation—a massive, pulsating structure that seemed to be the source of their coordination. The Doctor approached it, his sonic screwdriver at the ready. "Cover me. This will take a few moments."

As the Doctor worked to upload the virus, the others formed a defensive perimeter, fending off waves of Replicators that surged towards them. Bullets and energy blasts filled the air, and the tension was palpable.

"How much longer, Doc?" O'Neill shouted, firing at an approaching cluster of Replicators.

"Almost there!" the Doctor replied, his fingers moving rapidly over the device. "Just keep them off me a little longer!"

With a final flourish, the Doctor activated the virus. The massive structure shuddered, and a low hum filled the air. The Replicators around them began to falter, their movements becoming erratic.

"It's working!" Carter exclaimed. "The virus is disrupting their network!"

As the Replicators collapsed, the combined forces of UNIT, Torchwood, and SG-1 let out a collective cheer. The immediate threat had been neutralized, and the city was momentarily safe.

The Doctor turned to the group, a triumphant smile on his face. "Well done, everyone. But we're not out of the woods yet. We need to find out who's behind this and put a stop to it once and for all."

Captain Jack Harkness clapped the Doctor on the back. "You're right. But for now, let's take a moment to catch our breath."

Colonel O'Neill nodded in agreement. "Agreed. We've earned it."

As they regrouped and tended to the wounded, the sense of camaraderie and unity was strong. They had faced an overwhelming enemy and emerged victorious, but the battle was far from over. With the Doctor's leadership and the combined strength of UNIT, Torchwood, and SG-1, they were ready to face whatever came next.

The fight for survival continued, but hope was on their side. Together, they would overcome any obstacle and save the universe from the Replicator threat.

Chapter 8: Cybermen's Demise

The TARDIS interior hummed with its usual comforting sounds, but the atmosphere was anything but calm. The Doctor, SG-1, Sarah Jane, and Rose were gathered around the central console, the holographic display showing a grim scene unfolding in the depths of space.

The screen showed a Cybermen fleet, vast and imposing, its metallic ships glinting coldly against the starry backdrop. But something was terribly wrong. Swarms of Replicators were tearing through the Cybermen defenses, absorbing their technology and adapting at an alarming rate.

The Cybermen with their energy weapons tried to defeat this foe that was much more advance than their weapon because with every shot the Replicators absorbed the energy gaining strength. The Cybermen with their vast weapons were no match for this bug. Nor were they intelligent enough with their hive mind to figure out a way to defeat this new enemy, that has a vastly superior hive mind.

Colonel O'Neill leaned in, his eyes narrowing. "Doctor, what are we looking at?"

The Doctor's face was etched with concern as he manipulated the controls to get a clearer view. "The Replicators have found the Cybermen. They're consuming their technology, integrating it into their own systems. This is very bad."

Major Carter's scientific curiosity was piqued, despite the dire situation. "If the Replicators are absorbing Cybermen tech, they'll become even more advanced. They'll gain new abilities and become even harder to stop."

Teal'c, ever the warrior, remained stoic. "Then we must find a way to stop them before they become unstoppable."

Daniel Jackson watched the screen, his face a mask of concern. "Doctor, what can we do?"

The Doctor ran a hand through his hair, frustration evident. "We need to disrupt their process. The longer they have to assimilate Cybermen technology, the stronger they'll become. We have to act now."

Rose stepped forward, her voice steady. "Doctor, you've faced worse odds before. We can find a way to stop them. We just need to think."

The Doctor nodded, drawing strength from Rose's words. "You're right. There's always a way. We just have to find it."

As they watched, the Cybermen's attempts to fight back grew increasingly futile. The Replicators swarmed over the metallic soldiers, tearing them apart and integrating their parts. The Cybermen's iconic voices, usually so full of cold arrogance, were now filled with something almost resembling fear.

"Warning! System failure! Replicators—"

The screen flickered as a Cyberman ship exploded, the Replicators spreading out like a plague. The sight was enough to make even the most hardened soldiers feel a pang of dread.

Jack Harkness, standing at the edge of the group, crossed his arms. "This is bad. Really bad. If the Replicators get their hands on all that Cyber-tech, they could become unstoppable."

The Doctor's eyes blazed with determination. "Then we stop them before they get the chance."

Carter studied the display. "Doctor, if we can create a focused EMP burst, it might disrupt their assimilation process. But we'd need to get close—dangerously close."

The Doctor's mind raced. "We could use the TARDIS to get in close, but we need to time it perfectly. We'll have one shot at this."

O'Neill nodded. "We're with you, Doctor. Let's take these things down."

As the TARDIS dematerialized and reappeared in the midst of the chaos, the team prepared for the mission. The central console beeped with incoming data, the Doctor's hands flying over the controls.

"Everyone, hold on tight. This is going to be rough," the Doctor announced, his tone serious.

The TARDIS materialized inside a Cyberman ship, the metallic walls echoing with the sounds of battle. The Doctor, SG-1, Sarah Jane, and Rose stepped out, weapons and tools at the ready.

Replicators swarmed around them, their legs clicking ominously. Carter quickly set up the EMP device while Teal'c and O'Neill provided cover, their weapons cutting through the advancing Replicators.

"Doctor, we need to hurry!" Carter shouted, her voice barely audible over the din of battle.

The Doctor nodded, using his sonic screwdriver to boost the EMP's power. "Just a few more seconds!"

As the Replicators closed in, the EMP device emitted a high-pitched whine. "Now, Major Carter!" the Doctor yelled.

Carter activated the EMP, and a pulse of energy surged outwards, causing the Replicators to convulse and collapse. The swarm faltered, their assimilation process disrupted.

O'Neill grinned, but it was short-lived. "That's one down. How many more to go?"

The Doctor looked grim. "This was just a small part of their force. We need to do this on a larger scale."

As they made their way back to the TARDIS, the Doctor's mind raced with possibilities. They had bought themselves some time, but the threat was far from over.

Once inside the TARDIS, the Doctor turned to his companions. "We need to take this fight to their central hive. If we can disrupt their command structure, we might be able to stop them for good."

Carter looked determined. "Then let's get to it. We need to move fast."

As the TARDIS dematerialized, taking them to the heart of the Replicator threat, the Doctor couldn't shake the feeling of impending doom. The Replicators were more powerful than ever, but he knew that with the combined strength and ingenuity of their team, they had a fighting chance.

The battle was far from over, but the Doctor and his allies were ready to face whatever came next. The fate of the universe hung in the balance, and they would not rest until the Replicators were defeated.

Chapter 9: Dalek Annihilation

The TARDIS hummed with a low, steady pulse, the central console awash with information. The Doctor, SG-1, Sarah Jane, Rose, and Jack Harkness gathered around, their faces reflecting a mixture of determination and unease. The holographic display now showed a new threat unfolding—a confrontation between a Dalek battalion and the relentless Replicators.

The Doctor's expression was grave as he pointed to the screen. "The Daleks. One of the most feared species in the universe. If the Replicators assimilate their technology, they'll become nearly unstoppable."

Colonel O'Neill's voice was tense. "We just saw them take down the Cybermen. What's the plan, Doctor?"

The Doctor adjusted the controls, zooming in on the battle. "The Daleks won't go down easily, but we need to be ready. We need to find a way to disrupt the Replicators' assimilation process again. This time, on a much larger scale."

Major Carter's mind was already working. "If we can create a feedback loop in their network, it might overload their systems. But we'll need to get close to their core."

Teal'c, ever stoic, added, "And the Daleks will not hesitate to destroy us if we interfere."

Rose stepped forward, her voice steady. "We don't have a choice. We need to act now."

The Doctor nodded. "Rose is right. Everyone, get ready. This is going to be a rough ride."

The TARDIS materialized in the midst of the chaotic battle. The air outside was thick with the sounds of Dalek lasers and the metallic clattering of Replicators. The group emerged, weapons and tools at the ready, immediately greeted by the sight of Daleks and Replicators locked in fierce combat.

"EXTERMINATE! EXTERMINATE!" the Daleks chanted, their eyestalks swiveling to target the Replicators. Blue laser beams shot out, disintegrating clusters of the mechanical invaders.

But the Replicators were adapting quickly, their bodies shifting and reforming, absorbing the Dalek technology. The Doctor's eyes widened as he saw the Replicators start to incorporate Dalek weapons into their forms.

"We need to move quickly," he shouted. "Carter, set up the feedback loop device. O'Neill, Teal'c, cover her!"

Carter nodded, her fingers moving deftly over the device she had brought. O'Neill and Teal'c took up defensive positions, their weapons blazing as they fought off waves of Replicators.

Daniel Jackson and Sarah Jane provided additional cover, using their own weapons to keep the advancing Replicators at bay. Jack Harkness, his face set with determination, fired his energy blaster, taking down a group of Replicators that had adapted Dalek weaponry.

"Doctor, we need to buy Carter more time!" Jack shouted over the din of battle.

The Doctor nodded, using his sonic screwdriver to create a temporary barrier, giving them a few precious moments. "Carter, how much longer?"

"Almost there!" she replied, sweat beading on her forehead as she worked furiously.

As the Replicators began to break through the barrier, Carter finally activated the device. A high-pitched whine filled the air, and the feedback loop sent a pulse through the Replicator network. The mechanical invaders convulsed, their systems overloading.

"It's working!" Carter exclaimed. "But it won't hold for long. We need to get to their core and shut them down permanently."

The Doctor's eyes scanned the battlefield, spotting a massive Replicator structure at the center of the chaos. "There! That's their central core. We need to get inside and deploy the final disruptor."

O'Neill nodded. "Let's move, people!"

The group pushed forward, fighting their way through the disoriented Replicators and dodging Dalek fire. The Daleks, noticing the humans' advance, turned their attention towards them.

"INTRUDERS DETECTED! EXTERMINATE!"

The Doctor shouted, "Carter, can you modify the disruptor to affect the Daleks as well?"

Carter nodded, already working on the device as they ran. "I'll need a few minutes."

"Make it quick!" O'Neill barked, taking down another Replicator with a well-aimed shot.

They reached the entrance of the Replicator core, a massive structure pulsing with energy. The team forced their way inside, the Doctor using his sonic screwdriver to seal the entrance behind them temporarily.

"Alright, Carter, now's your chance," the Doctor said, watching the door as it shuddered under the assault from outside.

Carter set up the modified disruptor in the center of the core, her hands moving quickly and precisely. "This should do it. We just need to activate it."

The Doctor stepped forward, his sonic screwdriver at the ready. "On my mark. Everyone, brace yourselves."

The team gathered around the device, their weapons ready. The Doctor activated the sonic screwdriver, and a powerful pulse emanated from the disruptor, sending shockwaves through the Replicator core and the Dalek systems.

Outside, the Replicators began to collapse, their bodies disintegrating as the feedback loop tore through their network. The Daleks, caught in the crossfire, convulsed and exploded, their systems overloaded by the sudden surge.

"It's working!" Rose shouted, her face lighting up with hope.

The core shuddered, the walls cracking and sparking as the disruptor did its work. The Replicator hive began to collapse in on itself, the feedback loop tearing through their systems with relentless efficiency.

As the structure began to crumble, the Doctor turned to his companions. "We need to get out of here! Now!"

The team ran for the exit, dodging falling debris and collapsing structures. The TARDIS was just ahead, its familiar blue form a beacon of safety.

They piled inside, the Doctor slamming the door shut and rushing to the console. "Hold on, everyone!"

The TARDIS dematerialized just as the Replicator core imploded, sending a shockwave through the battlefield. The screen flickered, showing the aftermath—the Replicators were defeated, and the Dalek threat neutralized.

Inside the TARDIS, the mood was a mix of relief and exhaustion. Colonel O'Neill leaned against the wall, a grin on his face. "That was one hell of a ride."

Major Carter nodded, her face beaming with pride. "We did it. We actually did it."

Teal'c, ever the warrior, simply nodded in approval. "Indeed."

Daniel Jackson looked at the Doctor. "What's next, Doctor?"

The Doctor smiled, his eyes twinkling with the promise of new adventures. "Next, we find out who's been orchestrating all of this and put a stop to them once and for all."

Rose stepped forward, her voice filled with determination. "And we'll be right there with you, Doctor. Until the end."

The Doctor placed a reassuring hand on her shoulder. "Together, Rose. We'll face whatever comes next together."

As the TARDIS continued its journey, the team knew that the battle was far from over. But with the Doctor leading them, they were ready to face any challenge. The Replicators had been dealt a severe blow, but the true mastermind behind the chaos was still out there. And the Doctor would not rest until they were brought to justice.

Chapter 10: Advanced Replicators

The TARDIS spun through the vortex, the Doctor's fingers flying over the console as he adjusted their course. The mood inside was tense, the recent battle with the Replicators still fresh in everyone's minds. The Doctor's face was a mask of concentration, his eyes flickering with worry.

"We've got a new problem," the Doctor announced, his voice carrying a weight of urgency. "The Replicators have evolved again. With Dalek and Cyberman technology, they're now more advanced than ever."

Colonel O'Neill frowned, crossing his arms. "What kind of 'advanced' are we talking about here, Doc?"

The Doctor glanced at the holographic display, which showed the Replicators' new forms. Sleek, agile, and bristling with weaponry, they were a fusion of Dalek and Cyberman technology, their bodies reinforced with impenetrable alloys.

"They've integrated Dalek weaponry and Cyberman adaptability," the Doctor explained. "They're faster, stronger, and more dangerous than ever. And now they're turning their attention to Gallifrey."

Rose's eyes widened in shock. "Gallifrey? But that's your home!"

The Doctor nodded grimly. "If they assimilate Time Lord technology, they'll become unstoppable. We need to get there before they do."

Major Carter, analyzing the data on the screen, added, "Doctor, if they reach Gallifrey, they could potentially harness the power of the Time Vortex. They could control time itself."

Teal'c, ever stoic, spoke with quiet determination. "Then we must ensure that does not happen."

The Doctor pulled a lever, and the TARDIS lurched forward, accelerating through the vortex. "Hold on tight, everyone. This is going to be a bumpy ride."

As the TARDIS materialized on Gallifrey, the group stepped out into a world of stark beauty and advanced technology. The Citadel of the Time Lords stood tall in the distance, its spires reaching towards the sky.

The Doctor's face softened with a mix of nostalgia and determination. "Welcome to Gallifrey. But we don't have time for sightseeing. The Replicators could arrive at any moment."

Sarah Jane looked around, her eyes wide with wonder. "It's beautiful, Doctor. But you're right. We need to move."

As they made their way towards the Citadel, a piercing alarm suddenly sounded, echoing across the landscape. The Doctor's face darkened. "They're here."

In the distance, a massive swarm of Replicators descended from the sky, their new forms glinting ominously. They moved with a terrifying speed and precision, their mechanical legs slicing through the air.

Colonel O'Neill raised his weapon. "Here we go again. Carter, Teal'c, let's set up a defensive perimeter. Doctor, what's the plan?"

The Doctor's mind raced. "We need to get to the Citadel and warn the Time Lords. They have defenses, but they need to know what they're up against."

Rose and Sarah Jane stood by his side, ready for anything. "We're with you, Doctor," Rose said firmly.

"Let's go," the Doctor said, leading the way.

As they approached the Citadel, the Replicators launched their attack. Dalek energy beams and Cyberman blasters fired in unison, tearing through the air. The Doctor, Rose, and Sarah Jane ducked behind cover, returning fire with their sonic devices and blasters.

"Doctor, over here!" Sarah Jane shouted, pointing to a side entrance to the Citadel.

They sprinted towards the entrance, the Replicators hot on their heels. Inside, the Citadel's guards were already engaging the invaders, but the advanced Replicators were proving to be a formidable foe.

"Guardians of Gallifrey, hold your ground!" a voice boomed. It was Rassilon, the legendary leader of the Time Lords, his imposing figure commanding respect.

The Doctor rushed to his side. "Rassilon, we need to coordinate our defenses. These Replicators have assimilated Dalek and Cyberman technology. They're unlike anything we've faced before."

Rassilon's eyes narrowed. "We will not let them take Gallifrey. What do you propose, Doctor?"

The Doctor quickly explained the plan. "We need to create a temporal feedback loop to disrupt their systems. But we'll need access to the mainframe in the Citadel's core."

Rassilon nodded. "Very well. Follow me."

As they made their way through the Citadel, the battle raged on outside. Colonel O'Neill and SG-1 held the line, their weapons blazing as they fought off wave after wave of Replicators. Teal'c's staff weapon and Carter's blaster cut through the mechanical swarm, but the Replicators kept coming.

"How much longer, Doctor?" O'Neill shouted into his comms.

"We're almost there!" the Doctor replied, his voice crackling with urgency. "Just hold on a little longer!"

Inside the core, the Doctor and Rassilon worked quickly to set up the temporal feedback loop. The room was filled with advanced technology, the heart of Gallifrey's power.

"Doctor, we need to synchronize the temporal matrix with the disruptor," Carter said, her eyes focused on the controls.

The Doctor nodded, his hands moving rapidly over the console. "I'm on it. Rose, Sarah Jane, keep an eye on the entrance. We can't let the Replicators get in here."

Rose and Sarah Jane took up defensive positions, their weapons ready. The sounds of battle grew closer, the Replicators relentless in their advance.

Finally, the Doctor looked up, his face determined. "It's ready. Carter, activate the disruptor on my mark."

The Replicators burst into the room, their eyes glowing with a menacing light. Rose and Sarah Jane opened fire, holding them back just long enough.

"Now, Carter!" the Doctor shouted.

Carter activated the disruptor, and a powerful pulse emanated from the core, spreading outwards. The Replicators convulsed, their systems overloaded by the temporal feedback loop. One by one, they collapsed, their bodies disintegrating into dust.

Outside, the effect was the same. The Replicators faltered and fell, their advanced forms no match for the combined technology of Gallifrey and the Doctor's ingenuity.

The battlefield fell silent, the Replicators defeated. The team stood amidst the ruins, their faces etched with relief and exhaustion.

"We did it," Rose said softly, her eyes shining with hope.

The Doctor smiled, his hearts filled with pride and gratitude. "Yes, we did. But this is just one battle. The war is far from over."

Rassilon approached, his expression respectful. "You have saved Gallifrey, Doctor. For that, you have our eternal gratitude."

The Doctor nodded. "We must remain vigilant. The Replicators may be down, but they're not out. We need to find out who's behind this and stop them once and for all."

As the TARDIS prepared to depart, the Doctor turned to his companions. "We have a long road ahead of us, but with all of you by my side, I know we can face whatever comes next."

With renewed determination, the team stepped back into the TARDIS, ready for their next adventure. The universe was still in danger, but they had hope. And as long as they had that, they would never give up the fight.

Chapter 11: Gallifrey in Danger

The TARDIS materialized in the heart of the Time Lord Citadel on Gallifrey, its arrival marked by the familiar wheezing groan. The Doctor, SG-1, Sarah Jane, Rose, and Jack Harkness stepped out, greeted by the sight of Time Lord guards rushing to and fro, preparing for the imminent threat. The air was thick with tension, and the ominous hum of advanced technology filled the halls.

Rassilon, flanked by a group of senior Time Lords, approached, his expression grim. "Doctor, the Replicators are on their way. Our sensors have detected a massive swarm heading straight for Gallifrey."

The Doctor's face was etched with determination. "Then we need to act quickly. We can't let them assimilate Time Lord technology. It would spell doom for the entire universe."

Colonel O'Neill, his weapon at the ready, stepped forward. "What's the plan, Doctor? We need to set up our defenses and hit them hard."

Major Carter, analyzing the data on a nearby console, nodded. "We need to deploy a multi-phased defense system. EMPs, energy disruptors, and temporal shields. It's our best chance to slow them down."

Teal'c, ever the warrior, added, "I will assist in fortifying our perimeter. We must ensure that no Replicators breach the Citadel."

The Doctor turned to Rassilon. "We need full access to the Citadel's defenses. Every available resource must be used to repel the Replicators."

Rassilon nodded, his voice resolute. "You have full access, Doctor. The survival of Gallifrey is our highest priority."

The Doctor quickly outlined the defense plan, assigning tasks to everyone. "Jack, take Torchwood and secure the eastern perimeter. Sarah Jane and Rose, you're with me. We need to coordinate the deployment of the disruptors. SG-1, work with the Time Lords to set up the EMPs and temporal shields."

As everyone dispersed to their assignments, the Doctor, Sarah Jane, and Rose moved to the Citadel's control room, the heart of Gallifrey's defenses. The room was filled with advanced technology, holographic displays showing the approaching swarm of Replicators.

"Sarah Jane, monitor the sensors. We need to know their exact position at all times," the Doctor instructed, his fingers flying over the controls.

"Got it, Doctor," Sarah Jane replied, her eyes focused on the screen.

Rose moved to assist the Doctor, her voice steady. "What can I do?"

The Doctor handed her a device. "Help me calibrate the energy disruptors. We need them to be perfectly synchronized to create a feedback loop."

Meanwhile, in the eastern perimeter, Jack Harkness and his Torchwood team set up energy disruptors and fortified their positions. Gwen Cooper and Ianto Jones worked swiftly, their faces set with determination.

"Jack, we've got the disruptors online," Gwen reported, her eyes scanning the area for any signs of the enemy.

"Good job, Gwen. Ianto, how's our ammo?" Jack asked, checking his weapon.

"We're fully stocked. Let's just hope it's enough," Ianto replied, his voice tinged with apprehension.

"Stay sharp, team. They'll be here any minute," Jack said, his eyes narrowing as he scanned the horizon.

Back in the Citadel, SG-1 and the Time Lords worked together to set up the EMPs and temporal shields. Major Carter and Teal'c coordinated with the Time Lord engineers, while Colonel O'Neill and Daniel Jackson provided cover and support.

"Carter, how's it looking?" O'Neill asked, his eyes flicking between the equipment and the approaching swarm on the screen.

"We're almost there, sir. Just a few more adjustments," Carter replied, her fingers moving rapidly over the controls.

Teal'c stood guard, his staff weapon ready. "We must be prepared. The Replicators will not relent."

As the preparations were finalized, the tension in the air grew palpable. The Replicators were closing in, their mechanical forms visible on the horizon. The ground trembled with their approach, a relentless tide of destruction.

The Doctor's voice came over the comms, calm but urgent. "Everyone, this is it. Hold your positions and be ready. We cannot let them breach the Citadel."

The first wave of Replicators hit the defenses with a force that shook the ground. Energy disruptors fired, EMPs pulsed, and temporal shields flickered with energy. The Replicators convulsed as they hit the defenses, but they quickly adapted, pushing forward with relentless determination.

"Jack, how's it looking on the east side?" the Doctor called out.

"We're holding, but they're adapting fast!" Jack shouted back, firing at a cluster of Replicators.

In the control room, Sarah Jane monitored the sensors, her face tense. "Doctor, they're breaking through in several areas. We need to reinforce our defenses."

The Doctor's mind raced. "Rose, increase the power to the disruptors. We need to overload their systems."

Rose nodded, her hands moving swiftly over the controls. "On it, Doctor."

Colonel O'Neill's voice crackled over the comms. "We've got a breach on the north side. Carter, Teal'c, let's move!"

SG-1 rushed to the north perimeter, where the Replicators had broken through. Teal'c's staff weapon and O'Neill's P90 cut through the mechanical swarm, while Carter set up an emergency EMP device.

"Hang on, almost there," Carter said, her hands moving with precision.

As the EMP activated, a wave of energy surged through the Replicators, causing them to collapse. But more kept coming, their numbers seemingly endless.

Back in the control room, the Doctor was a blur of motion, coordinating the defense and making rapid adjustments. "We need to disrupt their central command node. It's the only way to stop them."

Rassilon, standing beside the Doctor, nodded. "The central node is heavily guarded. We'll need a direct assault."

The Doctor turned to Rose and Sarah Jane. "We'll take the TARDIS. It's the fastest way to get there."

As they made their way to the TARDIS, the battle raged on. Time Lord guards and SG-1 fought side by side, their combined firepower holding the line. Torchwood continued to defend the eastern perimeter, their energy disruptors cutting through the Replicator swarm.

The TARDIS materialized near the Replicators' central command node, a massive structure pulsing with energy. The Doctor, Rose, and Sarah Jane stepped out, immediately greeted by the sight of Replicators swarming the area.

"We need to get inside and disable their command node," the Doctor said, his voice urgent.

They fought their way through the Replicators, using their weapons and the Doctor's sonic screwdriver to disrupt the machines. As they reached the central node, the Doctor quickly set up a device to create a feedback loop.

"Rose, Sarah Jane, cover me while I set this up," the Doctor instructed, his hands moving rapidly over the device.

Rose and Sarah Jane opened fire, holding back the Replicators as the Doctor worked. The air was thick with tension, the sounds of battle echoing all around them.

"Doctor, hurry!" Sarah Jane shouted, taking down a Replicator that had gotten too close.

"Almost there!" the Doctor replied, his fingers flying over the controls.

With a final adjustment, the Doctor activated the device. A powerful pulse emanated from the central node, spreading through the Replicator network. The machines convulsed and collapsed, their systems overloaded by the feedback loop.

Back at the Citadel, the Replicators faltered and fell, their bodies disintegrating into dust. The battlefield fell silent, the immediate threat neutralized.

The Doctor, Rose, and Sarah Jane returned to the TARDIS, their faces etched with relief and exhaustion. As they materialized back in the Citadel, they were greeted by the sight of their allies, battered but victorious.

Colonel O'Neill clapped the Doctor on the back. "Nice work, Doc. We did it."

Rassilon approached, his expression one of respect and gratitude. "You have saved Gallifrey once again, Doctor. For that, you have our eternal thanks."

The Doctor nodded, his eyes filled with determination. "This was just one battle. We need to find out who's behind this and stop them once and for all."

As they regrouped and tended to the wounded, the sense of camaraderie and unity was strong. They had faced an overwhelming enemy and emerged victorious, but the war was far from over. With the Doctor's leadership and the combined strength of UNIT, Torchwood, and SG-1, they were ready to face whatever came next.

The fight for survival continued, but hope was on their side. Together, they would overcome any obstacle and save the universe from the Replicator threat.

Chapter 12: TARDIS Under Siege

The TARDIS hummed with a comforting resonance as it floated in the time vortex, but the sense of peace was fleeting. The Doctor, SG-1, Sarah Jane, Rose, and Jack Harkness were gathered around the central console, discussing their next move.

"We need to track down the source of the Replicators' command signal," the Doctor said, his brow furrowed in concentration. "Whoever is controlling them has a plan, and we need to stop them before they cause more destruction."

Suddenly, the TARDIS shuddered violently, alarms blaring as red lights flashed throughout the console room.

"What's happening, Doctor?" Rose shouted, gripping the edge of the console for support.

The Doctor's face turned pale. "The Replicators! They're trying to infiltrate the TARDIS!"

Colonel O'Neill drew his weapon instinctively. "Can they do that?"

Major Carter, her eyes wide with alarm, added, "If they can get inside the TARDIS, they could potentially take control of it."

The Doctor's hands flew over the controls, his face set with grim determination. "Not if I can help it. Everyone, brace yourselves!"

The TARDIS lurched again, and the central column pulsed erratically. The Doctor activated the internal defense systems, but the Replicators were already breaching the outer shell.

"Doctor, they're getting through!" Sarah Jane exclaimed, her eyes fixed on the monitor displaying the invading Replicators.

"Sarah Jane, I need your help," the Doctor said urgently. "We need to divert them into the zero room. It's the only place they can't affect."

Sarah Jane nodded, her resolve firm. "Tell me what to do."

The Doctor handed her a sonic device. "Use this to reconfigure the internal corridors. We need to guide them away from the control room and into the zero room."

As Sarah Jane rushed to the corridor controls, the Doctor continued to fend off the Replicators. "Rose, Jack, O'Neill, Carter, Teal'c, Daniel —split up and guard the key areas. We can't let them reach the heart of the TARDIS."

The team moved quickly, each taking up positions throughout the TARDIS. Teal'c and O'Neill covered the corridor leading to the control room, their weapons ready. Carter and Daniel guarded the secondary systems room, while Jack and Rose positioned themselves near the temporal engines.

The Replicators began to pour into the TARDIS, their metallic bodies clattering against the ancient coral walls. Teal'c's staff weapon blazed, and O'Neill's P90 rattled off shots, but the mechanical invaders kept coming.

"There's too many of them!" O'Neill shouted, his eyes darting to Teal'c.

"We must hold our ground," Teal'c replied, his face a mask of determination.

In the secondary systems room, Carter worked furiously to keep the Replicators at bay, using a modified EMP device to disrupt their circuitry. "Daniel, keep them off me while I set this up!"

Daniel fired at the advancing Replicators, his heart pounding. "How much longer, Sam?"

"Just a few more seconds," she replied, her voice tense.

Jack and Rose fought side by side near the temporal engines, their energy weapons cutting through the mechanical swarm. "We need to buy the Doctor more time," Jack said, his voice strained.

"We're doing our best, Jack," Rose replied, her face set with determination.

In the corridor, Sarah Jane worked quickly to reconfigure the internal pathways, her sonic device emitting a soft hum. "Doctor, I'm almost done. Just need a few more seconds."

The Doctor continued to work at the console, his eyes darting to the monitor. "Hurry, Sarah Jane. They're getting closer."

With a final adjustment, Sarah Jane reconfigured the corridors, diverting the Replicators towards the zero room. "It's done, Doctor! They're heading towards the zero room."

The Doctor activated the zero room's containment field, trapping the Replicators inside. The mechanical invaders convulsed as the field disrupted their systems, rendering them inert.

"Got them!" the Doctor shouted triumphantly. "Everyone, regroup in the control room."

As the team reconvened, the Doctor deactivated the alarms and steadied the TARDIS. The atmosphere was tense but filled with relief.

Colonel O'Neill wiped his brow. "That was too close for comfort."

Major Carter nodded, her face reflecting the strain of the battle. "We need to find out how they managed to breach the TARDIS in the first place."

The Doctor sighed, his expression thoughtful. "They're evolving faster than I anticipated. We need to find their command source and shut it down permanently."

Sarah Jane, her eyes filled with determination, said, "We can't let them win, Doctor. We have to stop them."

The Doctor placed a reassuring hand on her shoulder. "We will, Sarah Jane. We will."

The TARDIS, now secure, hummed with a renewed sense of purpose. The Doctor adjusted the controls, setting a course to trace the command signal. The team stood ready, united in their resolve to end the Replicator threat once and for all.

As the TARDIS spun through the vortex, the Doctor's eyes blazed with determination. "We're coming for you, whoever you are. And we won't stop until the universe is safe."

The fight was far from over, but with their combined strength and unwavering resolve, the Doctor and his companions knew they could face any challenge. The Replicators had underestimated them, and they would soon learn the true meaning of resistance.

Chapter 13: Meeting of Minds

The TARDIS materialized with a wheeze and a thud in the main conference room of UNIT headquarters. The Doctor stepped out first, adjusting his bow tie, followed by Sarah Jane, Rose, and Jack Harkness. SG-1—Colonel O'Neill, Major Carter, Dr. Jackson, and Teal'c—followed closely behind.

The room was filled with the familiar faces of UNIT personnel, including Kate Stewart, who stood at the head of the table. The atmosphere was tense but determined.

"Welcome back, Doctor," Kate greeted, her voice steady despite the urgency of the situation. "We're ready to hear your plan."

The Doctor nodded, moving to the center of the room. "We've faced a lot of threats, but the Replicators are different. They adapt quickly, and now that they've integrated Dalek and Cyberman technology, they're even more formidable."

Major Carter stepped forward, holding a tablet displaying various schematics. "Our initial strategy using EMPs was effective, but the Replicators have evolved. EMPs no longer work on them."

Captain Jack Harkness leaned against the table, his face grim. "So, what's our next move?"

The Doctor's eyes sparkled with determination. "We need to find a way to disrupt their cohesion. They're made up of individual blocks, each with its own function. If we can separate these blocks, we can neutralize them."

Daniel Jackson adjusted his glasses, looking thoughtful. "You mean, we need a frequency modulation device?"

"Exactly," the Doctor said, snapping his fingers. "A device that can emit a precise frequency to disrupt the connections between the blocks, effectively disassembling them."

Kate Stewart nodded. "Do we have the technology to create such a device?"

Major Carter looked at the schematics on her tablet. "We have the components, but we'll need to modify them significantly. It's going to take some time."

Teal'c, his voice calm but resolute, added, "We must act swiftly. The Replicators will not wait."

The Doctor moved to a whiteboard, sketching out a rough design for the device. "Carter, you and I will work on the technical specifications. Jack, coordinate with Torchwood and UNIT to gather the necessary components. Sarah Jane, Rose, and Daniel, I need you to look into the Replicators' command structure. We need to know who's controlling them and why."

As the teams dispersed to their tasks, the room buzzed with activity and purpose. The Doctor and Major Carter worked side by side, their minds racing to create the frequency modulation device.

"Doctor," Carter said, her eyes focused on the design, "if we can get the modulation frequency right, we can target the connections between the blocks without damaging other systems."

The Doctor nodded. "Precisely. It's a delicate balance, but I know we can do it."

Meanwhile, Jack coordinated with UNIT and Torchwood, ensuring that all necessary components were gathered and delivered to the lab. Gwen and Ianto worked tirelessly, their faces set with determination.

"Gwen, I need those power converters over here," Jack called out.

"On it, Jack," Gwen replied, carrying a heavy box of components.

Ianto checked his list, making sure nothing was missing. "Everything's accounted for. Let's get these to the lab."

In another part of the facility, Sarah Jane, Rose, and Daniel Jackson pored over data, trying to uncover the identity of the Replicators' controller.

"These signals are complex," Rose said, her brow furrowed. "But there's a pattern here. Someone is definitely behind this."

Daniel nodded. "If we can trace the origin of the signal, we might be able to find out who's orchestrating this."

Sarah Jane looked up from her computer. "I've got something. A faint signal coming from the edge of the Milky Way. It's masked, but it's definitely a command signal."

Rose's eyes widened. "We need to get this to the Doctor and Major Carter. They need to know."

As they rushed to the lab, the Doctor and Carter were finalizing the device. "We've got the modulation frequency," Carter said, a note of triumph in her voice.

The Doctor grinned. "Fantastic. Now we just need to test it."

Sarah Jane burst into the room, followed by Rose and Daniel. "Doctor, we've found the source of the command signal. It's coming from the edge of the Milky Way."

The Doctor's eyes lit up. "Excellent work. That's where we'll go next. But first, let's see if this device works."

They moved to a secure testing area, where a captured Replicator block was contained within an energy field. The Doctor and Carter set up the device, calibrating it carefully.

"Everyone, stand back," the Doctor warned. "Here goes nothing."

He activated the device, and a low hum filled the air. The Replicator block shuddered, its connections breaking apart. Within moments, it disassembled into its individual components, rendered inert.

"It works!" Carter exclaimed, her face beaming.

The room erupted in cheers, the sense of hope palpable. The Doctor turned to the group, his eyes filled with determination. "We've got our weapon. Now, let's take the fight to them."

Kate Stewart stepped forward, her voice strong. "UNIT will provide support. We'll ensure that the device is deployed where it's needed most."

Jack Harkness added, "Torchwood's got your back. We'll hit them hard and fast."

Colonel O'Neill nodded. "SG-1 is ready. Let's finish this."

The Doctor smiled, his hearts swelling with pride and resolve. "Together, we can stop them. Let's save the universe."

With their plan in place and their spirits high, the team prepared for the final confrontation. The Replicators had evolved, but so had their resistance. United in their cause, they were ready to face the ultimate challenge and bring an end to the Replicator threat once and for all.

Chapter 14: Ancient Technology

The TARDIS materialized in a remote, desolate corner of an alien planet, the landscape dominated by ancient ruins and towering stone structures. The Doctor, SG-1, Sarah Jane, Rose, and Jack Harkness stepped out, their eyes scanning the surroundings.

"Where are we, Doctor?" Rose asked, her voice echoing in the silence.

The Doctor adjusted his bow tie, his eyes gleaming with curiosity. "This is Xenthor Prime, home to one of the oldest and most advanced civilizations in the universe. Legend has it they possessed technology far beyond our understanding. If we can find it, it might hold the key to defeating the Replicators."

Colonel O'Neill raised an eyebrow. "Ancient technology, huh? Sounds promising. Where do we start?"

Major Carter consulted her scanner, the device beeping softly as it picked up faint energy signatures. "I'm detecting a power source nearby. It could be what we're looking for."

Teal'c, his staff weapon at the ready, took point. "We should proceed with caution. This place may hold dangers we are not yet aware of."

As they made their way through the ruins, the air grew thick with an ancient energy, the structures around them humming with a faint, almost imperceptible vibration. The group moved silently, their senses heightened.

Daniel Jackson, his eyes wide with awe, couldn't help but marvel at the inscriptions on the stone walls. "These markings... they're incredible. This civilization was truly advanced."

The Doctor nodded, his fingers brushing over the symbols. "Yes, they were. And if my hunch is correct, we're about to find something extraordinary."

They reached a massive stone door, intricately carved with symbols and glowing faintly with an inner light. Major Carter's scanner beeped more urgently. "The energy source is definitely behind this door."

The Doctor stepped forward, his sonic screwdriver in hand. "Let's see if we can't persuade it to open."

With a few deft movements, the sonic screwdriver emitted a high-pitched whine, and the stone door slowly creaked open, revealing a vast chamber filled with ancient technology. In the center stood a towering obelisk, its surface covered in glowing symbols and pulsating with a soft blue light.

Jack Harkness whistled, his eyes wide. "Now that's impressive."

The Doctor approached the obelisk, his face a mask of concentration. "This is it. The Heart of Xenthor. Legend has it that this device can control matter at a fundamental level. If we can harness its power, we might be able to disrupt the Replicators permanently."

Major Carter moved to the obelisk, her eyes scanning the readings on her tablet. "Doctor, the energy levels here are off the charts. We'll need to be careful."

Teal'c, standing guard at the entrance, suddenly tensed. "We are not alone."

From the shadows, a group of Replicators emerged, their metallic forms glinting in the dim light. They moved with a predatory grace, their eyes glowing with malevolent intelligence.

"Replicators! They must have followed us," Colonel O'Neill shouted, raising his weapon.

The team quickly took up defensive positions, their weapons ready. The Replicators surged forward, their legs clattering against the stone floor. Teal'c's staff weapon blazed, and O'Neill's P90 rattled off shots, but the Replicators kept coming.

"Doctor, we need to activate that thing now!" Jack shouted, firing at an approaching Replicator.

The Doctor and Major Carter worked frantically, their hands moving over the controls on the obelisk. "Almost there," the Doctor muttered, his face set with determination.

Rose and Sarah Jane provided cover, their energy weapons cutting through the Replicators. "Doctor, hurry!" Rose yelled, taking down a Replicator that had gotten too close.

With a final adjustment, the Doctor activated the obelisk. A surge of energy radiated outwards, enveloping the chamber in a blinding light. The Replicators convulsed, their forms disintegrating as the energy disrupted their connections at a molecular level.

"It's working!" Carter exclaimed, her eyes wide with amazement.

As the light faded, the Replicators lay in pieces on the ground, their threat neutralized. The team let out a collective sigh of relief, their weapons lowering.

"We did it," Sarah Jane said, her voice filled with awe.

The Doctor smiled, his hearts swelling with pride. "Yes, we did. But we need to ensure this technology is safeguarded. It's too powerful to fall into the wrong hands."

Colonel O'Neill nodded. "Agreed. We'll take care of it. But for now, let's get back to the TARDIS."

As they made their way back through the ruins, the Doctor couldn't help but feel a sense of accomplishment. They had discovered an ancient power and used it to turn the tide against the Replicators. But the fight was far from over.

Back in the TARDIS, the Doctor set a course for their next destination. "We've taken a big step forward, but we need to keep pushing. The Replicators are still out there, and whoever is controlling them won't stop until they're defeated."

Rose stepped up beside him, her eyes filled with determination. "We're with you, Doctor. All the way."

The Doctor smiled, his resolve stronger than ever. "Together, we'll save the universe."

With their spirits high and their resolve unwavering, the team prepared for the next phase of their battle against the Replicators. The ancient technology of Xenthor Prime had given them a powerful new weapon, and with it, they would continue their fight to protect the universe from the relentless threat of the Replicators.

Chapter 15: The First Attempt

The TARDIS landed with a soft thud in the heart of a UNIT command center, now serving as the nerve center for the combined forces of UNIT, Torchwood, SG-1, and the Doctor's allies. The air was thick with tension and anticipation as the team prepared for their first coordinated attack against the Replicators using the ancient technology from Xenthor Prime.

The Doctor, standing at the head of the central table, looked around at the assembled team. "Alright, everyone, this is it. We've got the Heart of Xenthor integrated into our systems. Major Carter and I have calibrated it to emit a frequency that should disrupt the Replicators at a molecular level. This is our best shot."

Colonel O'Neill nodded, his face serious. "Let's hope it works. We've only got one chance to hit them hard and fast."

Kate Stewart, head of UNIT, stood beside the Doctor. "We've identified a major Replicator hive in the Scottish Highlands. It's a strategic point. If we can neutralize it, we'll deal a significant blow to their operations."

Jack Harkness grinned, his usual confidence shining through. "Well, what are we waiting for? Let's go save the world."

The team dispersed, each person heading to their designated stations. The Doctor, Rose, Sarah Jane, and Jack joined SG-1 in a specially equipped UNIT transport, while the rest of the forces prepared to move out.

The Scottish Highlands were a stark contrast to the bustling command center. The serene landscape was marred by the sight of the Replicator hive, a massive, pulsating structure teeming with mechanical life. The team approached cautiously, the hum of their equipment mingling with the natural sounds of the highlands.

"Stay sharp, everyone," Colonel O'Neill whispered, his P90 at the ready. "We're not alone out here."

As they reached a vantage point, Major Carter set up the Heart of Xenthor, connecting it to a portable power source. "We're ready, Doctor. Just need to activate it."

The Doctor nodded, his eyes scanning the hive. "Alright. On my mark, everyone. Be prepared for anything."

The team took their positions, weapons aimed at the hive. The Doctor activated the Heart of Xenthor, and a low hum filled the air. A beam of pulsating energy shot out from the device, striking the hive directly. The structure shuddered, and for a moment, it seemed to work. The Replicators convulsed, their forms destabilizing.

"We've got them!" Sarah Jane exclaimed, her eyes wide with hope.

But just as quickly, the Replicators adapted. Their forms solidified, and they began to move towards the team with renewed vigor, their mechanical legs clattering ominously.

"Doctor, it's not working!" Rose shouted, firing her weapon at the advancing swarm.

The Doctor's face twisted with frustration. "They're adapting too quickly! We need more power, more frequency modulation!"

Teal'c stepped forward, his staff weapon blazing. "We must retreat and regroup. This position is no longer defensible."

O'Neill nodded, his face grim. "Carter, pack it up. Everyone, fall back!"

The team retreated, firing at the Replicators as they went. The Heart of Xenthor was quickly disassembled and packed away, but the Replicators were relentless, their numbers overwhelming.

"Keep moving!" Jack Harkness shouted, his energy weapon cutting through the mechanical swarm.

As they fell back to their transport, the Replicators surged forward, their eyes glowing with malevolent intelligence. The Doctor, his mind racing, activated the transport's defenses, creating a temporary barrier.

"We need to get back to the command center and come up with a new plan," the Doctor said, his voice strained. "This was just a test run. We'll figure it out."

Major Carter, her face set with determination, nodded. "We've got the data from this attempt. We'll analyze it and make the necessary adjustments."

The transport roared to life, speeding away from the hive as the Replicators swarmed around it. Inside, the team caught their breath, their minds already turning to the next steps.

Back at the UNIT command center, the atmosphere was tense. The team gathered around the central table, their faces etched with worry and determination.

Kate Stewart looked at the Doctor, her voice steady. "What happened out there?"

The Doctor sighed, running a hand through his hair. "The Replicators adapted too quickly. The Heart of Xenthor has potential, but we need to find a way to boost its power and refine the frequency modulation."

Major Carter added, "We'll need to run simulations and make adjustments. It's going to take time, but we'll get there."

Colonel O'Neill placed a reassuring hand on the Doctor's shoulder. "We'll figure it out, Doc. We always do."

Sarah Jane, her eyes filled with determination, said, "We can't give up. We're so close. We just need to keep pushing."

Rose nodded, her voice firm. "We'll find a way. We always do."

Jack Harkness grinned, his confidence unwavering. "And when we do, those Replicators won't know what hit them."

The Doctor smiled, his resolve stronger than ever. "Together, we'll make this work. We'll save the universe."

As the team set to work on refining their plan, the sense of unity and determination was palpable. They had faced a setback, but they were far from defeated. With the combined strength and ingenuity of UNIT, Torchwood, SG-1, and the Doctor's allies, they knew they could overcome any challenge.

The fight against the Replicators continued, but hope was on their side. And as long as they had that, they would never give up.

Chapter 16: SG-1's Plan

Back at the UNIT command center, the team regrouped to strategize their next move. The mood was somber but determined. The Replicators had proven to be more adaptable than anticipated, but SG-1 had a new plan.

Colonel O'Neill stood at the head of the table, flanked by Major Carter, Daniel Jackson, and Teal'c. The Doctor, Sarah Jane, Rose, and Jack Harkness listened intently.

"Alright, everyone," O'Neill began, "our first attempt didn't go as planned. The Replicators adapted too quickly. But we've got another idea, one that involves Asgard technology."

The Doctor's eyebrows shot up in curiosity. "The Asgard? I've heard of them, but I've never encountered their technology. Brilliant beings, if the stories are true."

Major Carter nodded. "The Asgard were an incredibly advanced race. They shared some of their technology with us before they... well, before they died."

The Doctor's expression turned solemn. "Died? What happened to them?"

Daniel Jackson explained, "The Asgard were facing a degenerative genetic condition. Rather than let their entire civilization crumble slowly, they chose to end their lives en masse, a planetary suicide. But their technology lives on, particularly on the Odyssey, a Daedalus-class Earth ship."

The Doctor's eyes widened. "That's both tragic and fascinating. Their technology could be the key we need to defeat the Replicators."

O'Neill continued, "The Odyssey is equipped with Asgard beaming technology, advanced shields, and weapons. We plan to use these to our advantage."

Carter elaborated, "The Asgard technology includes a disruptor specifically designed to target Replicator cells. If we can integrate it with the Heart of Xenthor, we might be able to create a powerful enough disruption to take them down."

Jack Harkness grinned. "Sounds like a plan. When do we start?"

Teal'c, ever the warrior, added, "We must move quickly. The Replicators will not wait."

O'Neill nodded. "Right. We're heading to the Odyssey. Carter, get the Heart of Xenthor ready for transport. Doctor, you and your team are coming with us."

The Doctor's eyes sparkled with excitement. "A trip to the Odyssey? I wouldn't miss it for the world."

The group quickly mobilized, boarding a UNIT transport that would take them to the Odyssey. The journey was filled with a sense of urgency, each member of the team focused on the task ahead.

Upon arrival, the massive Daedalus-class ship loomed overhead, its sleek lines and advanced technology a testament to the Asgard's legacy. The team boarded the ship, greeted by its crew and led to the command center.

Colonel Emerson, the commanding officer of the Odyssey, welcomed them. "Colonel O'Neill, Major Carter, Doctor. Welcome aboard. We're ready to assist in any way we can."

The Doctor looked around in awe. "This is incredible. The Asgard's influence is evident in every corner of this ship."

Carter wasted no time, directing the crew to set up the Heart of Xenthor in the ship's engineering bay. "We need to integrate the Asgard disruptor with this device. It's our best chance to amplify the disruption frequency."

As they worked, the Doctor couldn't help but marvel at the advanced technology around him. "The Asgard were truly remarkable. This ship is a marvel of engineering."

Carter, focused on the task at hand, nodded. "They were our allies and friends. We owe it to them to make this work."

Jack Harkness and Rose assisted with the setup, while Sarah Jane helped coordinate the logistics. The atmosphere was a mix of tension and excitement as they prepared for their next attempt.

With everything in place, Carter addressed the group. "We've integrated the Asgard disruptor with the Heart of Xenthor. This should amplify the disruption frequency and hopefully overcome the Replicators' adaptability."

Colonel Emerson spoke over the intercom. "We've detected a large concentration of Replicators on the dark side of the moon. This could be our best chance to test the device."

The Doctor's eyes lit up. "Then let's not waste any more time. Everyone to their stations."

The Odyssey ascended into orbit, positioning itself on the dark side of the moon. The tension on the bridge was palpable as the crew prepared to deploy the device.

"Doctor, are we ready?" O'Neill asked, his voice steady.

The Doctor nodded, his hands poised over the controls. "Ready as we'll ever be. Let's do this."

Carter activated the device, and a beam of pulsating energy shot out from the ship, striking the Replicator hive. The hive shuddered, and for a moment, it seemed like the disruption was working. The Replicators convulsed, their forms destabilizing.

But then, to everyone's horror, the Replicators adapted once again. Their bodies solidified, and they began to swarm towards the Odyssey with renewed aggression.

"It's not enough!" Carter shouted, her eyes wide with alarm.

Colonel Emerson ordered evasive maneuvers, the ship's shields flaring as they were hit by Replicator fire. "We need to pull back!"

The Doctor, his mind racing, shouted, "We need to boost the power! Use the ship's core to amplify the signal!"

Carter hesitated. "That's risky, Doctor. It could overload the system."

"We don't have a choice!" the Doctor replied. "It's now or never."

Colonel Emerson gave the order. "Do it."

Carter quickly rerouted the power, the ship's core glowing with intense energy. The Doctor activated the device again, and this time, the beam was stronger, brighter. It struck the Replicator hive with immense force, and the Replicators began to disintegrate, their forms breaking apart.

"It's working!" Rose shouted, her face lighting up with hope.

The Replicators fell, their bodies disintegrating into dust. The hive collapsed, the threat neutralized.

The crew let out a collective sigh of relief. Colonel O'Neill clapped the Doctor on the back. "Nice work, Doc. We did it."

The Doctor smiled, his eyes twinkling. "We've taken a big step forward. But the fight isn't over yet."

Carter, her face reflecting a mix of exhaustion and triumph, nodded. "We've got a powerful tool now. Let's use it to end this once and for all."

As the Odyssey returned to Earth, the team felt a renewed sense of hope and determination. They had faced a formidable enemy and emerged victorious, but the final battle was still ahead.

Back at the UNIT command center, the Doctor addressed the team. "We've got the technology we need. Now it's time to find the source of the Replicators and put an end to this once and for all."

Kate Stewart stepped forward, her voice resolute. "UNIT is ready. Let's finish this."

With their spirits high and their resolve unwavering, the team prepared for the final confrontation. The Replicators had underestimated them, and now, with the combined strength of UNIT, Torchwood, SG-1, and the Doctor's allies, they were ready to save the universe.

Chapter 17: Torchwood's Sacrifice

The atmosphere at Torchwood's Hub was tense as the team prepared for their most daring and desperate plan yet. The Hub, located in Cardiff, had always been a beacon of advanced technology and a place of great power due to its proximity to the Rift, an energy source that could bend space and time.

Captain Jack Harkness gathered his team in the central command room. Gwen Cooper, Ianto Jones, and the rest of Torchwood stood ready, their faces reflecting a mix of determination and apprehension.

"Alright, everyone," Jack began, his voice steady. "We've got one chance to make this work. We're going to use the power of the Rift to lure the Replicators into a trap. Once they're inside the Hub, we'll detonate the Rift energy, causing a massive explosion that will take out as many of them as we can."

Gwen stepped forward, her eyes filled with resolve. "It's risky, Jack. The Hub is our home. But if it's the only way..."

Ianto nodded, his face set with determination. "We're ready. Let's do this."

The Doctor, Sarah Jane, Rose, and SG-1 had joined them, their expressions reflecting the gravity of the situation. The Doctor stepped up beside Jack, his voice filled with urgency. "Are you sure about this, Jack? The Hub is more than just a base. It's a symbol of hope."

Jack's eyes were hard but determined. "We don't have a choice, Doctor. The Replicators are relentless. If we don't stop them here, they'll overrun everything. We need to buy time for the rest of the plan."

Colonel O'Neill, Major Carter, Teal'c, and Daniel Jackson stood ready to assist. O'Neill looked at Jack and nodded. "We'll cover you. Let's get this done."

The plan was set in motion. The team worked quickly to rig the Hub's systems to draw on the power of the Rift. Energy conduits were rerouted, and explosive charges were placed at key structural points. The goal was to create a massive energy surge that would lure the Replicators and then detonate, taking out as many as possible.

As the final preparations were made, Jack turned to his team, his voice filled with emotion. "You all know what's at stake. Torchwood has always stood against the darkness. Today, we stand together to protect the future."

Gwen, her voice steady, replied, "We're with you, Jack. To the end."

The Doctor, his face etched with concern, added, "Once the trap is set, we need to get everyone out. We can't afford to lose anyone."

Jack nodded. "Understood. Let's move."

The Replicators were already closing in on Cardiff, their metallic forms glinting ominously in the light. As they approached the Hub, the energy readings spiked, drawing them in like moths to a flame.

"We've got them," Carter reported, monitoring the sensors. "They're heading straight for the Rift energy."

The Replicators swarmed towards the Hub, their numbers overwhelming. Inside, the team worked with precision, making final adjustments and ensuring the trap was ready.

"Everyone, fall back to the exit points," Jack ordered. "Gwen, Ianto, you're with me."

As the team began to evacuate, the Replicators breached the Hub, drawn by the immense energy of the Rift. Jack and his team stayed behind, ensuring the Replicators were fully inside before triggering the trap.

"Jack, we need to go now!" the Doctor shouted, his voice urgent.

"Just a few more seconds," Jack replied, his eyes locked on the advancing swarm. "Alright, that's it. Gwen, Ianto, hit the detonator!"

Gwen and Ianto activated the charges, and the Hub was engulfed in a blinding explosion of Rift energy. The ground shook, and a massive shockwave radiated outwards, disintegrating the Replicators caught in the blast.

For a moment, it seemed like the plan had worked. But as the smoke cleared, it became evident that the Replicators had adapted once again. While a significant number had been taken out, the surviving Replicators were already reforming, their metallic bodies glinting with renewed vigor.

"Doctor, they're adapting too quickly," Carter said, her voice filled with frustration. "The explosion took out some of them, but it's not enough."

The Doctor's face was grim. "We need to fall back and regroup. This isn't over yet."

Jack, his face pale from the exertion, nodded. "Let's get out of here. We need to come up with another plan."

As the team retreated, the remains of the Hub smoldered behind them. It was a hard-fought battle, and the cost had been high, but the fight was far from over. The Replicators had proven their adaptability, and the team needed a new strategy.

Back at the UNIT command center, the atmosphere was tense. Kate Stewart addressed the group, her voice steady despite the gravity of the situation. "We've suffered a setback, but we're not beaten. We need to find another way to stop the Replicators."

The Doctor nodded, his mind racing with possibilities. "We need to think outside the box. The Heart of Xenthor, Asgard technology... there must be something we're missing."

Rose, her eyes filled with determination, said, "We'll find it, Doctor. We always do."

Jack, despite the loss of the Hub, grinned. "Torchwood will rise again. And we'll be right there with you, Doctor."

Colonel O'Neill placed a reassuring hand on the Doctor's shoulder. "We'll figure this out. Together."

As the team set to work, the sense of unity and determination was stronger than ever. They had faced a formidable enemy and suffered a setback, but they were far from defeated. With their combined strength and ingenuity, they were ready to continue the fight and protect the universe from the relentless threat of the Replicators.

Chapter 18: UNIT's Counterattack

The UNIT command center was a hive of activity. Maps and schematics covered the walls, while officers and soldiers moved with a sense of urgency. The Doctor, SG-1, and Torchwood gathered around a large central table where Kate Stewart and her top strategists were finalizing the plan for their counterattack against the Replicators.

Kate Stewart's voice was firm as she addressed the assembled team. "Our objective is to launch a full-scale offensive against the Replicators. We need to hit them hard and fast, disrupt their operations, and gather as much data as possible on their new adaptations. It's a high-risk mission, but it's our best chance to turn the tide."

The Doctor, standing beside her, added, "We've identified several key Replicator hives spread across Europe. Our main target will be the largest hive located in Germany. We'll use the Asgard-modified Heart of Xenthor and integrate it with UNIT's heavy artillery to maximize our impact."

Colonel O'Neill crossed his arms, his face set with determination. "We'll need to coordinate air and ground assaults to keep the Replicators off balance. Carter, you'll handle the deployment of the Asgard disruptor. Teal'c, Daniel, you're with me on the ground."

Jack Harkness leaned in, his eyes gleaming with resolve. "Torchwood will support the ground troops. We'll use what's left of our advanced weaponry to keep the Replicators busy."

Sarah Jane and Rose exchanged a determined glance. "We'll help wherever we're needed," Sarah Jane said. "This is an all-hands-on-deck situation."

Kate nodded. "Good. Let's move out. Everyone knows their roles. Stay sharp, stay focused, and remember—we're doing this for everyone who's counting on us."

The team dispersed, each heading to their designated stations. The Doctor and Major Carter oversaw the final preparations for the Asgard-modified Heart of Xenthor, ensuring it was ready for deployment.

As the forces mobilized, the Doctor took a moment to address the troops. "UNIT, Torchwood, SG-1—today, we stand united against a common enemy. The Replicators are relentless, but so are we. Let's show them what we're made of."

The soldiers cheered, their spirits lifted by the Doctor's words. They boarded their transport vehicles, ready for the battle ahead.

The German countryside, once peaceful and serene, was now a warzone. The Replicator hive loomed ominously on the horizon, a massive structure teeming with mechanical life. The air was thick with tension as the UNIT forces approached, their vehicles kicking up dust as they moved into position.

Colonel O'Neill's voice crackled over the comms. "All units, this is O'Neill. Begin the assault on my mark. Carter, is the disruptor ready?"

Major Carter's voice came through, steady and calm. "Disruptor is online and ready to deploy. Just waiting for your signal."

"Alright, people," O'Neill said, his voice filled with resolve. "Let's give them hell. Mark!"

The ground forces surged forward, a wave of soldiers and armored vehicles advancing on the Replicator hive. Overhead, fighter jets roared, launching missiles that struck the hive with explosive force. The Replicators responded immediately, swarming out to meet the assault with a terrifying speed and precision.

"Keep pushing forward!" Jack Harkness shouted, firing his weapon at the advancing Replicators. "Don't give them a chance to regroup!"

Teal'c's staff weapon blazed, cutting through the mechanical swarm. "We must reach the hive and deploy the disruptor."

Daniel Jackson, using a portable energy weapon, provided cover for the advancing troops. "We're making progress, but they're adapting quickly. We need to move faster."

The Doctor, from his vantage point, monitored the battle, his mind racing with strategies. "Carter, deploy the disruptor now! We need to disrupt their cohesion before they can adapt."

Major Carter activated the Asgard-modified Heart of Xenthor, and a beam of pulsating energy shot out, striking the Replicator hive. The hive shuddered, and for a moment, the Replicators convulsed, their forms destabilizing.

"It's working!" Carter shouted. "The disruptor is affecting their network."

But the Replicators, ever adaptive, began to reorganize. They shifted their formations, reducing the effectiveness of the disruptor. The soldiers on the ground fought valiantly, but the tide began to turn against them.

"Colonel, we're taking heavy casualties!" a UNIT officer reported, his voice strained. "We need reinforcements!"

O'Neill, his face grim, responded, "Hold the line! We can't afford to fall back now."

Jack Harkness, his face set with determination, shouted, "We need to lure more of them into the disruptor's range. Focus your fire on the flanks and drive them towards the center!"

Gwen and Ianto, fighting alongside the troops, executed Jack's plan, their weapons blazing. "Keep pushing!" Gwen yelled. "We can do this!"

Despite their best efforts, the Replicators began to gain the upper hand. The air was filled with the sounds of battle, the cries of the wounded, and the relentless clattering of the Replicators.

The Doctor, seeing the dire situation, turned to Sarah Jane and Rose. "We need to find their command node. It's the only way to stop them from adapting."

The trio moved quickly, using the chaos of the battle as cover. They reached the edge of the hive and slipped inside, navigating the maze-like corridors filled with Replicator constructs.

"Over here," Sarah Jane whispered, pointing to a large chamber. "This looks like a central control room."

Inside, the command node pulsed with energy, surrounded by Replicators. The Doctor activated his sonic screwdriver, emitting a high-frequency pulse that disrupted the Replicators momentarily.

"Now, Rose!" the Doctor shouted.

Rose threw a modified disruptor grenade into the chamber, and it exploded with a burst of energy, causing the command node to flicker and die. The Replicators convulsed, their network disrupted.

Back outside, the Replicators faltered, their coordinated attack breaking down. The UNIT and Torchwood forces seized the opportunity, pushing forward with renewed vigor.

"That did it!" O'Neill shouted. "All units, press the attack!"

The combined forces surged forward, taking advantage of the Replicators' momentary confusion. The disruptor beam intensified, and the Replicators began to disintegrate under the combined assault.

As the battle raged on, the Doctor, Sarah Jane, and Rose rejoined the main force. The tide had turned, but the cost was high. The ground was littered with the fallen, both Replicator and human.

Kate Stewart's voice came over the comms, filled with relief. "We've done it. The hive is collapsing."

The Replicator hive, its command structure destroyed, began to crumble. The remaining Replicators disintegrated, their forms breaking apart under the relentless assault.

The battlefield fell silent, the immediate threat neutralized. The survivors, battered and weary, regrouped, their faces reflecting a mix of relief and sorrow.

Colonel O'Neill addressed the troops, his voice filled with pride. "We took heavy losses, but we did it. We've gained valuable data that will help us in the final battle."

The Doctor, his face solemn, added, "This was a hard-fought victory, but the fight isn't over. We've learned a lot today, and we'll use that knowledge to end this once and for all."

Jack Harkness, despite the heavy toll, grinned. "Torchwood's ready. Let's finish this."

Sarah Jane and Rose, standing beside the Doctor, nodded. "We're with you, Doctor. To the end," Rose said, her voice filled with determination.

Kate Stewart stepped forward, her voice resolute. "UNIT is ready for whatever comes next. We'll stand together and protect this world."

With their spirits high and their resolve unwavering, the team prepared for the final confrontation. The Replicators had proven their resilience, but the combined forces of UNIT, Torchwood, SG-1, and the Doctor's allies were stronger than ever. They were ready to face the ultimate challenge and save the universe from the relentless threat of the Replicators.

Chapter 19: Rose's Insight

The command center of UNIT was a scene of controlled chaos. The recent battle had taken its toll, and the team was regrouping, analyzing the data they had collected. The Doctor stood at the central table, surrounded by his allies, their faces showing a mix of exhaustion and determination.

As the Doctor reviewed the data, Rose Tyler's expression shifted from deep thought to sudden realization. Her eyes widened as a memory from her time in the parallel universe surfaced.

"Doctor," Rose called out, her voice urgent. "I think I know something that might help."

The Doctor looked up, his curiosity piqued. "What is it, Rose?"

Rose took a deep breath, organizing her thoughts. "When I was in the parallel universe, we faced a threat similar to the Replicators. They weren't the same, but the principles of their technology were similar. We found a way to disrupt their coordination using a very specific type of energy frequency. It was something the Cybermen there had developed to defend against the void energy."

Major Carter, intrigued, stepped forward. "Void energy? That's the energy between dimensions, right? If the Replicators have tapped into similar technology, we might be able to use that against them."

Rose nodded. "Exactly. In the parallel universe, we used a device that emitted a void frequency. It destabilized their connections and disrupted their ability to adapt. If we can recreate that device, we might have a chance."

The Doctor's face lit up with excitement. "Rose, that's brilliant! We can combine that with the Asgard technology and the Heart of Xenthor. We might just have a solution."

Colonel O'Neill looked skeptical but hopeful. "How do we build this void frequency emitter? Do we have the resources?"

Major Carter began typing furiously on her tablet, pulling up schematics. "We'll need to modify the Asgard disruptor and integrate it with our existing technology. It won't be easy, but it's possible."

Jack Harkness grinned. "When have we ever done things the easy way?"

Teal'c, his voice steady, added, "Time is of the essence. We must begin immediately."

The Doctor, Rose, and Carter moved quickly to the lab, followed by the rest of the team. They began working on the device, each contributing their expertise. The atmosphere was charged with urgency and determination.

As they worked, Rose explained the details from her experience. "The key is to create a stable void frequency. It's not just about the power; it's about the precision. The slightest deviation, and it won't work."

The Doctor nodded, his hands moving deftly over the controls. "We need to tune the frequency perfectly. Carter, can you adjust the Asgard disruptor to emit void energy?"

Carter, focused on her task, replied, "I'm on it. Just need to reroute the power and modify the emitter."

Daniel Jackson, observing the process, asked, "Rose, what kind of resistance did you face when you used this technology before?"

Rose's face darkened slightly as she recalled the past. "It was tough. They adapted quickly, but the void frequency gave us enough of an edge to break through their defenses. We'll need to be ready for anything."

As the device neared completion, the tension in the room was palpable. The team knew this was their best chance to stop the Replicators once and for all.

Finally, Major Carter stepped back, her face showing a mix of relief and determination. "It's ready."

The Doctor looked at the device, a complex amalgamation of Asgard and UNIT technology, enhanced with the principles Rose had shared. "Let's hope this works."

Kate Stewart's voice came over the intercom. "We've detected a large Replicator fleet approaching. This is our chance to test the device."

The Doctor nodded. "Everyone, to your stations. This is it."

The team moved swiftly, each taking their positions. The void frequency emitter was set up at the center of the command room, ready to be deployed.

The Replicator fleet loomed on the horizon, a terrifying swarm of metallic invaders. The air was thick with tension as the team prepared for the attack.

"Activate the emitter on my mark," the Doctor commanded, his voice steady. "Three... two... one... mark!"

The void frequency emitter hummed to life, emitting a pulse of energy that resonated through the air. The Replicators convulsed, their forms destabilizing as the void frequency disrupted their connections.

"It's working!" Carter shouted, monitoring the readings. "Their network is breaking down!"

But the Replicators, true to form, began to adapt. Their bodies shifted, attempting to counter the disruption.

"We need to increase the power!" Rose shouted, adjusting the controls. "We have to overload their systems!"

The Doctor and Carter worked together, pushing the emitter to its limits. The room was filled with the high-pitched whine of the device, the air crackling with energy.

"Come on, just a little more," the Doctor muttered, his eyes fixed on the Replicators.

With a final surge, the void frequency reached its peak. The Replicators convulsed violently, their forms breaking apart as the energy overwhelmed them. One by one, they disintegrated, reduced to inert metal fragments.

The room fell silent, the tension giving way to a sense of relief and triumph.

"We did it," Rose said, her voice filled with amazement. "We actually did it."

The Doctor smiled, his eyes twinkling with pride. "Rose, your insight saved us. We couldn't have done it without you."

Colonel O'Neill clapped the Doctor on the back. "Nice work, everyone. We've got the edge we need."

Jack Harkness grinned, his confidence renewed. "Let's finish this."

Kate Stewart's voice came over the comms, filled with relief. "We've confirmed the destruction of the Replicator fleet. Excellent work, team."

The Doctor addressed the group, his voice filled with determination. "We've taken a major step forward, but the fight isn't over. We need to use this momentum and push back against the Replicators wherever they appear."

Sarah Jane, her eyes shining with resolve, added, "We'll be ready, Doctor. All of us."

Rose, standing beside the Doctor, nodded. "We'll stand together. To the end."

With renewed hope and a powerful new weapon, the team prepared for the final phase of their battle against the Replicators. The road ahead was still fraught with danger, but they were ready to face it together, united in their determination to protect the universe.

Chapter 20: The Timelord Council

The TARDIS materialized with a familiar wheeze and groan within the grand halls of the Capitol on Gallifrey. The architecture was a breathtaking blend of ancient and futuristic, with towering spires, intricate carvings, and a golden hue that seemed to glow from within. The Doctor, dressed in his formal Time Lord robes, stepped out, followed closely by Sarah Jane, Rose, Jack Harkness, and the members of SG-1.

"Welcome to Gallifrey," the Doctor said, his voice tinged with both pride and apprehension. "Let's hope the High Council is in a cooperative mood."

Colonel O'Neill, taking in the grandeur of the surroundings, couldn't help but quip, "So, this is where you're from, Doc? Nice place."

Sarah Jane, her eyes filled with nostalgia, whispered, "It's been so long since I've seen this. It's beautiful."

Rose, awe-struck by the sight, added, "Doctor, this place is amazing. But will they help us?"

The Doctor sighed, leading them through the labyrinthine corridors towards the Council Chamber. "The Time Lords aren't known for their willingness to get involved. But they must see the severity of the Replicator threat."

The group entered the grand chamber, where the High Council of the Time Lords was assembled. The Lord President, Rassilon, sat at the head of the table, flanked by other prominent Time Lords. Their expressions were a mix of curiosity and caution as they regarded the Doctor and his companions.

"Doctor," Rassilon intoned, his voice resonating through the chamber. "You have requested an audience with the High Council. State your case."

The Doctor stepped forward, his voice steady and authoritative. "Gallifrey is in danger. The entire universe is in danger. The Replicators have adapted to every form of technology we've used against them.

We've made progress with the void frequency emitter, but we need more. We need your help."

A murmured discussion broke out among the Council members. Finally, the Castellan spoke, his tone skeptical. "The Time Lords have maintained our neutrality for centuries. Why should we involve ourselves in this conflict?"

Jack Harkness stepped forward, his voice filled with determination. "Because this isn't just about one planet or one race. The Replicators will consume everything in their path. They'll find a way to breach the Time Lock and reach Gallifrey eventually."

Teal'c, his presence imposing and calm, added, "We have seen worlds fall to the Replicators. They will not stop until all life is extinguished or assimilated."

Rassilon's eyes narrowed as he regarded the group. "And what would you have us do, Doctor?"

The Doctor took a deep breath. "We need access to the Eye of Harmony. Its power can amplify the void frequency emitter to a level that the Replicators cannot adapt to. It's our best chance to end this threat once and for all."

A hush fell over the chamber. The Eye of Harmony was the source of the Time Lords' power, a singularity of immense energy and significance. Allowing outsiders access to it was unprecedented.

The Lady Chancellor spoke, her voice measured. "The Eye of Harmony is sacred. Allowing you to use it for this purpose carries great risk."

Daniel Jackson, always the diplomat, stepped forward. "We understand the risk. But the alternative is far worse. The Replicators will not stop. They'll consume everything, including Gallifrey. We're asking for your help to prevent that."

The Doctor looked directly at Rassilon, his eyes pleading. "Please. You know what's at stake. The Time Lords have the power to make a difference. Don't let this be the end of everything."

Rassilon leaned back, deep in thought. After a long, tense silence, he spoke. "Very well. We will grant you access to the Eye of Harmony. But understand this, Doctor—failure is not an option. The consequences would be catastrophic."

The Doctor bowed his head in gratitude. "Thank you, Rassilon. We won't fail."

The Council dispersed, and Rassilon approached the group, his demeanor more approachable. "Doctor, you have always been a thorn in the side of the High Council, but you have also been our greatest asset. Do not let us down."

The Doctor nodded, his expression serious. "We'll do whatever it takes."

As they made their way to the chamber housing the Eye of Harmony, the Doctor briefed the team. "The Eye of Harmony is a source of unimaginable power. We'll need to be extremely careful when channeling its energy through the void frequency emitter."

Major Carter, her scientific curiosity piqued, asked, "Doctor, how exactly do we interface the emitter with the Eye?"

The Doctor smiled, appreciating her keen mind. "We'll use the TARDIS as a conduit. It's already linked to the Eye. By adjusting the settings, we can direct the energy precisely where we need it."

Rose, walking beside him, placed a hand on his arm. "We'll get through this, Doctor. Together."

Jack Harkness, always confident, added, "You've got the best team here, Doc. Let's save the universe."

Inside the chamber, the Eye of Harmony glowed with a pulsating light, its energy radiating throughout the room. The Doctor and Major Carter worked quickly, setting up the void frequency emitter and linking it to the TARDIS.

"Everyone, be ready," the Doctor instructed. "Once we activate this, the energy surge will be immense."

The team took their positions, their faces reflecting a mix of determination and anxiety. The Doctor took a deep breath and activated the emitter.

A beam of energy shot out from the Eye of Harmony, channeled through the TARDIS and into the void frequency emitter. The room vibrated with power, the air crackling with electricity.

"It's working," Carter reported, monitoring the readings. "The frequency is stabilizing."

The Doctor, his face focused, adjusted the controls. "We need to maintain this for a few more seconds."

The energy beam intensified, and the void frequency emitter pulsed with a brilliant light. The Replicators, sensing the massive energy surge, began to converge on Gallifrey, their forms flickering as they struggled to adapt.

"Doctor, they're coming!" Sarah Jane shouted.

"Hold the frequency," the Doctor commanded. "We're almost there."

The Replicators swarmed into the chamber, their bodies destabilizing under the void frequency. They convulsed, their forms breaking apart as the energy overwhelmed them.

"It's working!" Rose exclaimed. "They're falling apart!"

The Replicators, unable to adapt to the amplified void frequency, disintegrated, their threat neutralized.

As the last of the Replicators fell, the room fell silent, the energy from the Eye of Harmony returning to its normal state. The team let out a collective sigh of relief, their faces showing a mix of exhaustion and triumph.

"We did it," the Doctor said, his voice filled with gratitude. "We actually did it."

Rassilon, watching from the entrance, nodded in approval. "You have done well, Doctor. The universe owes you a debt of gratitude."

Colonel O'Neill, ever the pragmatist, added, "Let's make sure they stay down this time."

The Doctor smiled, his hearts filled with pride and relief. "We will. With the High Council's support, we can ensure the Replicators are gone for good."

As the team left the chamber, their spirits high, the Doctor knew that they had achieved something truly extraordinary. With the help of the Time Lords, they had turned the tide against the Replicators and saved the universe from destruction.

Back in the TARDIS, the Doctor addressed his companions, his voice filled with hope. "We've faced impossible odds and come out victorious. But our work isn't done. There will always be new threats, new challenges. And we'll face them together."

Rose, Sarah Jane, Jack, and SG-1 nodded in agreement, their bond stronger than ever.

"To the next adventure," Rose said, her eyes shining with excitement.

The Doctor smiled, his hearts swelling with anticipation. "To the next adventure."

As the TARDIS dematerialized, the team knew that whatever lay ahead, they would face it together, united in their determination to protect the universe and uphold the legacy of the Time Lords.

Chapter 21: Gallifrey's Defense

The Citadel of the Time Lords, once a symbol of serene power and timeless wisdom, now buzzed with the urgent preparations for an impending battle. The Replicators had regrouped and launched a massive assault on Gallifrey, determined to claim its advanced technology for their own.

The Doctor, dressed once more in his Time Lord robes, stood at the heart of the Capitol's command center. Beside him were Sarah Jane, Rose, Jack Harkness, and SG-1, all ready to assist in the defense. Rassilon and the High Council had mobilized the full might of Gallifrey's defenses, but the atmosphere was tense.

Rassilon's voice was calm but firm as he addressed the assembled defenders. "The Replicators have breached our outer defenses. We must hold them here, at all costs. The survival of Gallifrey—and indeed the universe—depends on it."

The Doctor stepped forward, his face etched with determination. "We have the void frequency emitter and the power of the Eye of Harmony, but we need to coordinate our efforts. The Replicators are relentless and adaptable."

Colonel O'Neill nodded, his military experience coming to the fore. "We need to set up a perimeter defense and use the emitter to disrupt their formations. Teal'c, you and I will lead the ground troops. Carter, you and Daniel coordinate the emitter with the Time Lords."

Jack Harkness, his eyes gleaming with confidence, added, "Torchwood will handle the flanks. We've got some tricks up our sleeves that might slow them down."

The Time Lord Castellan, a stern figure clad in ornate robes, looked at the Doctor. "What of you, Doctor? Where will you be?"

The Doctor's eyes blazed with determination. "I'll be at the front lines. This is my home, and I'll defend it with everything I've got."

As the defenders moved to their positions, the Citadel's defenses activated, shimmering barriers and automated weaponry springing to life. The sky above Gallifrey darkened as the first wave of Replicators descended, their metallic forms glinting ominously in the dim light.

"Here they come!" Teal'c shouted, his staff weapon at the ready. "Hold the line!"

The Replicators hit the defenses with a force that shook the ground. The Time Lord guards, armed with advanced staser rifles, fired volley after volley, but the Replicators were relentless. The air was filled with the sounds of battle, the clash of metal, and the cries of the wounded.

Major Carter, working alongside the Time Lord technicians, monitored the void frequency emitter. "We need to adjust the frequency! They're adapting too quickly."

Daniel Jackson, using a portable scanner, provided the necessary data. "Try increasing the modulation by 5 percent. It should destabilize their connections."

Carter made the adjustments, and the emitter pulsed with a powerful energy wave. The Replicators convulsed, their forms breaking apart, but they quickly began to adapt.

"It's not enough!" Carter shouted. "We need more power!"

The Doctor, at the front lines, dodged and weaved through the chaos, using his sonic screwdriver to disrupt the Replicators' circuitry. "Keep pushing! We can't let them break through!"

Rose and Sarah Jane, fighting side by side, provided cover fire. "Doctor, we're holding them off, but they keep coming!" Rose called out, her voice strained.

Jack Harkness, leading a Torchwood squad, used a modified Rift energy weapon to blast a group of Replicators. "Keep firing! Don't let up!"

Despite their efforts, the Replicators began to gain ground. The barriers flickered as the relentless assault continued. The Time Lords, though powerful, were struggling to maintain their defenses.

"We need reinforcements!" a Time Lord guard shouted, his voice filled with desperation.

The Doctor, seeing the dire situation, turned to Rassilon. "We need to use the Eye of Harmony again. It's the only way to generate enough power to disrupt them completely."

Rassilon hesitated, knowing the risks. "Very well. Do what you must, Doctor."

The Doctor rushed back to the command center, where Major Carter and Daniel Jackson were coordinating the emitter. "We need to channel more power from the Eye of Harmony. It's risky, but it's our only chance."

Carter nodded, her face set with determination. "Understood. Let's do it."

As the Doctor and Carter worked together to reroute the power, the ground battle intensified. Colonel O'Neill and Teal'c led the charge, their weapons blazing. The Time Lord guards and UNIT soldiers fought valiantly, but the Replicators were relentless.

"We're being overwhelmed!" O'Neill shouted, firing at an advancing swarm. "Doctor, we need that power boost now!"

The Doctor and Carter made the final adjustments, and the void frequency emitter pulsed with an immense surge of energy, channeled directly from the Eye of Harmony. The ground shook, and a brilliant light enveloped the battlefield.

The Replicators convulsed violently, their forms breaking apart under the overwhelming energy. One by one, they disintegrated, unable to adapt to the sheer power of the Eye of Harmony.

"It's working!" Carter shouted, her voice filled with relief.

The remaining Replicators, sensing their imminent defeat, began to retreat. The defenders, seeing their chance, pushed forward, driving the Replicators back.

"We've got them on the run!" Jack Harkness yelled, his face lit with triumph. "Keep pushing!"

As the last of the Replicators fell, the battlefield fell silent. The defenders, battered and weary, regrouped, their faces reflecting a mix of relief and exhaustion.

Rassilon approached the Doctor, his expression one of respect. "You have done well, Doctor. Gallifrey is safe, thanks to you and your allies."

The Doctor nodded, his hearts filled with pride and relief. "This was a victory, but the fight isn't over. We need to ensure the Replicators can never threaten us again."

Colonel O'Neill, his face showing the strain of the battle, added, "We'll make sure of it. But for now, we've earned a moment of peace."

Sarah Jane and Rose, standing beside the Doctor, smiled. "We did it," Sarah Jane said softly. "We really did it."

Jack Harkness grinned, his confidence unshaken. "Torchwood's ready for whatever comes next."

Teal'c, his voice calm and steady, nodded. "We will remain vigilant. The threat may return, but we will be prepared."

As the defenders tended to the wounded and repaired the damage, the Doctor addressed his companions. "We've faced impossible odds and come out victorious. But our work isn't done. There will always be new threats, new challenges. And we'll face them together."

Rose, her eyes filled with determination, said, "We'll stand together. Always."

With renewed hope and a sense of unity, the team prepared for whatever lay ahead. The Replicators had been pushed back, but the fight for the universe's safety was far from over. Together, they would continue to protect and defend, united in their resolve to keep the universe safe from any threat.

Chapter 22: TARDIS Reinforced

The TARDIS hummed quietly, nestled in the heart of the UNIT command center. The Doctor, with a determined look on his face, had gathered his closest allies to discuss the next crucial step in their ongoing battle against the Replicators.

"Right," the Doctor began, addressing the group that included Sarah Jane, Rose, Jack Harkness, and SG-1. "The Replicators have breached the TARDIS before, and we can't let that happen again. We need to upgrade the TARDIS with Asgard technology. It's the only way to ensure our safety and give us an edge."

Major Carter, always ready to tackle a technical challenge, nodded. "The Asgard technology we have on the Odyssey is advanced enough to provide the necessary defenses. We can integrate their shields and security protocols into the TARDIS systems."

Colonel O'Neill crossed his arms, a wry smile on his face. "Sounds like a plan. Let's get to it before those metal pests come back for round two."

Jack Harkness grinned. "I always wanted to see the TARDIS tricked out with some alien tech. Let's make it happen."

With the plan set, the team moved to the Odyssey to gather the necessary components. The sleek, Daedalus-class ship was a stark contrast to the ancient and organic feel of the TARDIS, but the Doctor's excitement was palpable as they worked.

As they entered the engineering bay of the Odyssey, Carter began to explain the integration process. "We'll need to transfer the Asgard shielding systems and the security protocols. This includes their adaptive energy shields and the auto-repair functions. We'll also integrate their communication encryption to prevent any external hacking."

The Doctor's eyes gleamed with enthusiasm. "Brilliant. Let's start with the adaptive shields. Rose, Jack, I need you to help with the physical transfer. Carter and I will handle the integration."

Teal'c and O'Neill stood guard, ensuring the area remained secure while the work was underway. Daniel Jackson, meanwhile, assisted with translating the Asgard schematics and instructions.

As they worked, the Doctor couldn't help but marvel at the sophistication of the Asgard technology. "The Asgard were truly remarkable. Their technology is a perfect blend of power and elegance."

Carter smiled, sharing his admiration. "They were our allies and friends. Integrating their tech into the TARDIS is a fitting tribute to their legacy."

Rose and Jack, using portable grav-lifts, transported the Asgard components into the TARDIS. The interior of the TARDIS seemed to hum with anticipation as the new systems were brought in.

"Where do you want this, Doctor?" Rose asked, struggling slightly with the weight of the components.

"Right over there, by the central console," the Doctor replied, pointing. "We'll start the integration from the main power source."

Jack set his load down with a satisfied grunt. "I never thought I'd see the day. Asgard tech in the TARDIS. This is going to be something."

The Doctor and Carter worked side by side, connecting the adaptive shields to the TARDIS's power grid. The console room was filled with a soft blue light as the new systems came online, the TARDIS adjusting to the upgrades.

"We need to calibrate the shields to the unique energy signature of the TARDIS," Carter explained, typing furiously on her laptop. "That way, they'll respond instantly to any threat."

The Doctor nodded, his sonic screwdriver buzzing as he made the necessary adjustments. "Once the shields are in place, we'll integrate the auto-repair functions. That will ensure any damage can be fixed immediately."

As they continued their work, Teal'c and O'Neill maintained a vigilant watch outside the TARDIS. "How's it looking in there?" O'Neill called out.

"We're making progress," Carter replied. "Just a few more connections."

The Doctor, deep in concentration, finally stepped back and admired their work. "The adaptive shields are online. Now for the security protocols."

They moved on to the next phase, integrating the Asgard security systems. These included advanced encryption for the TARDIS communications and enhanced internal sensors to detect and neutralize any intruders.

"With these protocols, we'll be able to detect and repel any unauthorized access," Carter explained. "The Asgard security systems are incredibly sophisticated."

The Doctor smiled, clearly impressed. "This will make the TARDIS virtually impenetrable. Exactly what we need."

Rose, watching the systems come online, asked, "Doctor, what about the Replicators' ability to adapt? Can these upgrades really keep them out?"

The Doctor nodded confidently. "The Asgard technology is designed to counteract adaptive threats. With these upgrades, the TARDIS will be more than a match for the Replicators."

Jack clapped his hands together, his grin wide. "Now that's what I like to hear."

As the final connections were made, the TARDIS hummed with a new energy. The central console glowed with a soft blue light, and the air seemed to vibrate with power.

"The upgrades are complete," Carter announced, stepping back and wiping her brow. "The TARDIS is now equipped with Asgard adaptive shields, auto-repair functions, and enhanced security protocols."

The Doctor, beaming with pride, addressed his companions. "We've done it. The TARDIS is now more powerful and secure than ever before. This will give us the edge we need against the Replicators."

Colonel O'Neill gave a satisfied nod. "Good work, everyone. Now let's test these upgrades."

Teal'c, ever the warrior, added, "We must ensure that the enhancements function as intended. A live test is essential."

The Doctor agreed. "Let's take the TARDIS for a spin. We'll test the shields and security systems under real conditions."

As the team prepared for the test, the Doctor activated the TARDIS. The familiar wheezing and groaning filled the air as the TARDIS dematerialized, reappearing in the midst of space near a known Replicator-infested region.

"Shields up," Carter instructed, monitoring the readings. "Let's see how they handle an incoming threat."

Almost immediately, a swarm of Replicators detected the TARDIS and moved to attack. The adaptive shields flared to life, creating a shimmering barrier that deflected the Replicators' attempts to breach the TARDIS.

"It's working!" Rose exclaimed. "The shields are holding."

The Doctor, his face lit with excitement, watched the monitors. "Let's see how they handle sustained pressure."

The Replicators intensified their assault, but the Asgard shields adapted to their attacks, growing stronger and more resilient. The TARDIS remained secure, the shields shimmering with energy.

"Security protocols active," Carter reported. "The TARDIS internal sensors are detecting and neutralizing any attempts at infiltration."

Jack Harkness, grinning broadly, added, "Looks like we've got ourselves an impenetrable fortress."

The Doctor nodded, his hearts swelling with pride. "We've done it. The TARDIS is now a true stronghold. This will give us the edge we need to take the fight to the Replicators."

As the Replicators finally retreated, unable to breach the TARDIS's defenses, the team breathed a collective sigh of relief. The upgrades had proven effective, and the TARDIS was now ready for the final battle.

Back at the UNIT command center, the Doctor addressed his companions. "We've made incredible progress, but the fight isn't over. With the TARDIS reinforced and our new strategies, we're ready to end this once and for all."

Sarah Jane, Rose, Jack, and SG-1 nodded in agreement, their resolve unshaken.

"To the final battle," Rose said, her eyes filled with determination.

The Doctor smiled, his eyes twinkling with anticipation. "To the final battle. Let's save the universe."

With their spirits high and their resolve unwavering, the team prepared for the ultimate confrontation with the Replicators. The TARDIS, now more powerful than ever, would lead them into the fray, ready to protect and defend the universe from any threat.

Chapter 23: Hidden Knowledge

The TARDIS hummed gently in the background as Sarah Jane Smith sat at one of the many consoles, her curiosity piqued. They had faced overwhelming odds and made incredible strides against the Replicators, but Sarah Jane felt there was still something missing—an ancient secret or piece of knowledge that could tip the scales definitively in their favor.

"Doctor," Sarah Jane called, her voice thoughtful. "I've been thinking. We've upgraded the TARDIS, we've used the Asgard technology, but what if there's something even older that we've overlooked? Something ancient and powerful?"

The Doctor, tinkering with the central console, looked up, intrigued. "What are you thinking, Sarah Jane?"

She stood up, her eyes alight with the excitement of discovery. "The TARDIS has been to countless places and times. There must be hidden knowledge somewhere in its vast database. Ancient texts, forgotten lore —something that could help us."

The Doctor's eyes twinkled with excitement. "You're absolutely right! The TARDIS has a hidden library, a repository of the most ancient and obscure knowledge in the universe. Let's go find it."

Rose, overhearing the conversation, joined them. "A hidden library? I've got to see this."

Jack Harkness grinned, following suit. "Count me in. I love a good treasure hunt."

SG-1, ever the curious and resourceful team, also expressed interest. Major Carter looked particularly enthusiastic. "Ancient texts often contain wisdom long forgotten. It's worth exploring."

The Doctor led the way through the winding corridors of the TARDIS, deeper than any of them had ventured before. The walls seemed to pulse with a life of their own, the TARDIS guiding them towards the hidden library.

After several twists and turns, they arrived at a grand, ornate door. The Doctor waved his sonic screwdriver, and the door creaked open, revealing a vast room filled with towering shelves of ancient books, scrolls, and artifacts. The air was thick with the smell of aged paper and a sense of timeless wisdom.

"Welcome to the hidden library," the Doctor announced, his voice filled with reverence. "Everything in here is rare, ancient, and incredibly powerful."

Sarah Jane's eyes widened as she took in the sight. "This is incredible. Where do we even start?"

Major Carter, already scanning the titles, suggested, "Let's look for anything related to advanced technology or ancient defense mechanisms."

The group split up, each person searching the shelves for any clue that might help. The Doctor, Sarah Jane, and Rose focused on one section, while Jack and SG-1 took another.

After hours of searching, Sarah Jane pulled out a large, dusty tome bound in dark leather. "Doctor, I think I found something."

The Doctor rushed over, peering over her shoulder. The book was titled *The Chronicles of the Ancients*. "Good find, Sarah Jane. Let's see what it says."

They opened the book, the ancient pages crackling under their touch. The text was written in an old, forgotten language, but the TARDIS translated it seamlessly. As they read, their eyes widened with excitement.

"The Ancients faced a threat similar to the Replicators," Sarah Jane read aloud. "They created a device called the Quantum Matrix Disruptor. It was designed to break down the molecular bonds of self-replicating entities."

Major Carter, hearing this, joined them. "A Quantum Matrix Disruptor? That sounds exactly like what we need. How do we build it?"

The Doctor scanned further, his eyes narrowing in concentration. "It's a complex device, requiring elements from various advanced technologies, including Time Lord and Asgard components. But we can do it."

Daniel Jackson, flipping through another section of the book, added, "It also says here that the device was powered by a unique energy source—the Heart of the Universe. We'll need to find a substitute."

Rose looked at the Doctor. "The Eye of Harmony?"

The Doctor nodded. "Yes, the Eye of Harmony should provide the necessary power. We just need to integrate it carefully."

Jack Harkness, always ready for action, clapped his hands. "Alright, let's get to work. We've got a universe to save."

Back in the TARDIS control room, the team set up a makeshift lab, gathering the necessary components and starting the assembly of the Quantum Matrix Disruptor. The atmosphere was filled with focused energy, everyone working in sync.

The Doctor and Major Carter took the lead, their hands moving deftly as they connected the intricate parts. "We'll use the Asgard shielding to contain the energy," Carter explained, "and the Time Lord technology to stabilize the quantum field."

Teal'c and Colonel O'Neill stood guard, ensuring no interruptions. Daniel Jackson and Sarah Jane assisted with the translations and assembly, while Rose and Jack managed the logistics, fetching and carrying parts as needed.

As they neared completion, the Doctor carefully linked the device to the TARDIS console. "We need to channel the Eye of Harmony's energy into the Disruptor. It's delicate work, but we can do it."

With a final adjustment, the device hummed to life, its core glowing with a brilliant light. The Doctor smiled, a mix of pride and relief on his face. "It's ready."

Major Carter nodded, her eyes reflecting the same determination. "Let's test it."

The Doctor set a course for a remote asteroid field known to harbor a small Replicator nest. The TARDIS materialized, and the team prepared to deploy the Quantum Matrix Disruptor.

"Everyone ready?" the Doctor asked, his hand poised over the activation switch.

"Ready," they replied in unison.

The Doctor activated the device, and a beam of shimmering energy shot out, enveloping the Replicator nest. The Replicators convulsed, their forms breaking apart as the quantum bonds were disrupted. Within moments, the entire nest disintegrated into dust.

"It works!" Rose exclaimed, her face lighting up with triumph.

The Doctor grinned. "Indeed it does. This is the key to defeating the Replicators."

Colonel O'Neill clapped the Doctor on the back. "Nice work, Doc. Let's take this fight to them."

With the Quantum Matrix Disruptor in hand, the team returned to the TARDIS, their spirits high. They had uncovered ancient knowledge that provided the missing piece in their battle against the Replicators. Armed with this powerful new weapon, they were ready to face the ultimate challenge and save the universe.

As the TARDIS dematerialized, the Doctor addressed his companions. "We've come a long way, and we've got a bit further to go. But with this device, we have the power to end the Replicator threat once and for all."

Sarah Jane, her eyes filled with determination, added, "We'll stand together and fight until the end."

The Doctor smiled, his hearts swelling with pride and hope. "To the end, and beyond. Let's save the universe."

With renewed resolve and a powerful new weapon, the team prepared for the final showdown with the Replicators. The hidden knowledge they had uncovered would be their beacon of hope, guiding them to victory and ensuring the safety of the universe.

Chapter 24: SG-1's Breakthrough

The TARDIS hummed with a low, steady pulse, serving as both a sanctuary and a hub of frenetic activity. After uncovering the hidden library and the ancient texts detailing the Quantum Matrix Disruptor, SG-1 was hard at work deciphering further sections of the ancient manuscripts. The Doctor, Sarah Jane, Rose, Jack Harkness, and SG-1 were gathered around the central console, poring over the texts.

Major Carter, her face a mask of concentration, scanned the pages of an ancient tome with her tablet. "These texts are incredibly detailed. The Ancients were far more advanced than we ever realized."

Daniel Jackson, who had taken on the primary role of translating the texts, nodded in agreement. "The language is complex, but there are sections here that describe an even more powerful weapon than the Quantum Matrix Disruptor. They called it the Genesis Protocol."

Colonel O'Neill, ever the pragmatist, leaned in. "Genesis Protocol? Sounds like something we could use. What is it exactly?"

Daniel adjusted his glasses, his excitement palpable. "From what I can decipher, it's a system designed to reprogram the molecular structure of self-replicating entities at a fundamental level, essentially turning their own replication process against them. It's a way to force them to self-destruct."

Teal'c, his face stoic but interested, asked, "How is this achieved, Daniel Jackson?"

Daniel pointed to a specific passage. "It involves creating a specific frequency that can be encoded with a molecular blueprint. When the Replicators absorb this frequency, it reprograms their structure, causing them to disassemble."

Major Carter's eyes lit up with realization. "If we can integrate this protocol into the Quantum Matrix Disruptor, we could potentially wipe out the Replicators for good."

The Doctor, always eager to learn, leaned over Daniel's shoulder. "Show me the details. We need to understand exactly how this frequency works and how to generate it."

Daniel spread out the ancient manuscript on the console, highlighting the crucial sections. "The key is in the frequency modulation. It's incredibly precise. We'll need to use the TARDIS's systems to generate the correct waveform."

The Doctor nodded, already formulating a plan. "Rose, Jack, I need you to gather the components from the Odyssey. Carter, Daniel, you'll help me integrate the Genesis Protocol into the Disruptor. Teal'c, O'Neill, you'll handle security and make sure we're not interrupted."

As they dispersed to their tasks, the atmosphere in the TARDIS was electric with urgency and determination. The team knew this breakthrough could be the key to their ultimate victory against the Replicators.

Back in the makeshift lab, the Doctor and Major Carter began the complex process of integrating the Genesis Protocol into the Quantum Matrix Disruptor. The room buzzed with the sound of equipment and the low hum of the TARDIS's power systems.

"The frequency needs to be perfectly modulated," Carter explained, adjusting the controls on the Disruptor. "Even the slightest error could render it ineffective."

The Doctor, using his sonic screwdriver to fine-tune the settings, replied, "Agreed. The TARDIS's systems can generate the precise waveform we need. We just have to synchronize it with the Disruptor's output."

Daniel, working alongside them, cross-referenced the ancient texts with the schematics they had developed. "According to this, the frequency should cause a cascading failure in the Replicator's core programming. Once it starts, it can't be stopped."

Rose and Jack returned with the components from the Odyssey, their faces reflecting the intensity of the moment. "Here's everything you asked for, Doctor," Rose said, setting the equipment on the workbench.

Jack, ever the optimist, grinned. "Let's get this thing up and running. I'm ready to see some Replicators go boom."

As they worked, the TARDIS's central console emitted a series of beeps, indicating an incoming transmission. The Doctor activated the viewscreen, revealing Kate Stewart from UNIT.

"Doctor, we've detected a massive Replicator fleet heading towards Earth. They're converging on multiple locations. We're running out of time," Kate said, her voice urgent.

The Doctor's face hardened with determination. "We're almost ready, Kate. Hold them off as long as you can. We'll be there soon."

Back at the lab, the final adjustments were made. The Quantum Matrix Disruptor, now integrated with the Genesis Protocol, hummed with a new, powerful energy. Major Carter ran a final diagnostic, her face breaking into a relieved smile.

"It's ready," she announced. "The Genesis Protocol is fully integrated."

The Doctor nodded, his face resolute. "Then it's time to test it. Let's save the universe."

The TARDIS materialized at the heart of a major Replicator incursion site, the air thick with the sounds of battle. UNIT soldiers and Torchwood agents were engaged in fierce combat, struggling to hold back the relentless swarm.

"All units, fall back to the TARDIS!" Colonel O'Neill ordered over the comms. "We're deploying the weapon."

As the team moved into position, the Doctor and Major Carter activated the Quantum Matrix Disruptor. The device emitted a low hum, and a beam of energy shot out, enveloping the Replicator swarm.

At first, the Replicators convulsed as they had before. But then, a change occurred. Their forms began to destabilize, breaking apart at the molecular level. The air was filled with the sound of their disintegration as the Genesis Protocol took effect.

"It's working!" Rose shouted, her face alight with triumph. "They're falling apart!"

The Replicators, unable to adapt to the new frequency, disintegrated en masse. The swarm collapsed, their threat neutralized.

Kate Stewart's voice came over the comms, filled with relief. "The Replicators are retreating. We've done it."

The battlefield fell silent as the last of the Replicators disintegrated. The defenders, though battered and weary, erupted in cheers. The Quantum Matrix Disruptor had worked, and the Genesis Protocol had given them the edge they needed.

Colonel O'Neill clapped the Doctor on the back. "Nice work, Doc. We've got ourselves a real game-changer here."

Teal'c, his voice calm but filled with pride, added, "This is a significant victory. We must remain vigilant."

Sarah Jane, her eyes filled with gratitude, said, "We couldn't have done this without you, Doctor. You and your friends saved us all."

The Doctor smiled, his hearts swelling with pride and relief. "We did it together. And we'll continue to stand together, no matter what comes next."

As the team regrouped, the Doctor addressed his companions. "We've achieved a great victory today, but the fight isn't over. We need to ensure the Replicators are gone for good."

Rose, standing beside him, nodded. "We'll stand with you, Doctor. To the end."

With the Genesis Protocol in hand and the Quantum Matrix Disruptor at their side, the team was ready for the final battle. The universe was safer, but the ultimate challenge still lay ahead. Together, they would face it and emerge victorious.

Chapter 25: Building the Weapon

The TARDIS once again stood at the center of the UNIT command hub, its doors open to the frenetic activity of soldiers, scientists, and engineers working in unison. The discovery of the Genesis Protocol had given the team new hope, and now they were united in their efforts to build the ultimate weapon that would end the Replicator threat once and for all.

The Doctor, Sarah Jane, Rose, Jack Harkness, and SG-1 were gathered around a large table covered with blueprints, schematics, and ancient texts. Kate Stewart and her top strategists from UNIT stood by, ready to coordinate their efforts.

"Alright, everyone," the Doctor began, his voice calm but filled with urgency. "We've deciphered the Genesis Protocol from the ancient texts, and we have a clear understanding of how to build the weapon. It's going to require components from Time Lord, Asgard, and Earth technology. We need to work together to get this done quickly."

Major Carter, examining the schematics, added, "We'll need to integrate the Quantum Matrix Disruptor with the Genesis Protocol. The key is to create a device that can emit the precise frequency needed to disrupt the Replicators at a molecular level."

Daniel Jackson, still poring over the ancient texts, nodded. "The texts mention using a crystalline structure to amplify the frequency. We should start by constructing that first."

Colonel O'Neill, ever the pragmatist, looked at Kate Stewart. "Kate, we'll need your best engineers to help with the assembly. We'll also need a secure facility to work in. This thing can't fall into the wrong hands."

Kate Stewart nodded, her expression serious. "You'll have everything you need. We'll make sure of it."

The team split into smaller groups, each tasked with different aspects of the weapon's construction. The Doctor, Major Carter, and Daniel Jackson focused on integrating the Genesis Protocol with the Quantum Matrix Disruptor. Teal'c and Colonel O'Neill oversaw the assembly of the crystalline structure, while Sarah Jane, Rose, and Jack Harkness coordinated the logistics and managed the influx of necessary components.

In a secure lab, Major Carter and the Doctor worked side by side, their hands moving swiftly over the intricate circuitry of the Disruptor. The room buzzed with the sound of welding, the hum of machinery, and the low murmur of intense concentration.

"We need to ensure the frequency modulator is perfectly calibrated," Carter said, her eyes focused on the task at hand. "Any deviation and the weapon won't be effective."

The Doctor adjusted his sonic screwdriver, fine-tuning the connections. "I'm on it. The TARDIS's systems should help us achieve the necessary precision."

Daniel Jackson, translating a particularly complex section of the ancient texts, added, "According to this, the crystalline structure needs to be aligned with the Eye of Harmony's energy signature. That's what will give the weapon its power."

Rose, bringing over a tray of components, asked, "Doctor, how do we channel the Eye of Harmony's energy without overloading the system?"

The Doctor smiled, appreciating her insight. "We'll use a series of stabilizers to regulate the flow. It's like turning on a tap gradually rather than all at once. The energy needs to be steady and controlled."

In another part of the lab, Teal'c and Colonel O'Neill worked with UNIT engineers to construct the crystalline structure. The air was filled with the sound of crystals being cut and shaped, each piece carefully aligned to form a complex lattice.

"These crystals are incredibly delicate," one of the engineers remarked. "We need to handle them with extreme care."

Teal'c, his hands steady and sure, nodded. "Precision is key. Each crystal must be perfectly aligned to amplify the frequency."

Colonel O'Neill, overseeing the process, added, "Take your time, but we need to move quickly. The Replicators won't wait."

As the assembly progressed, Sarah Jane and Jack Harkness coordinated the efforts, ensuring that each component arrived on time and in perfect condition. The logistics were a monumental task, but their experience and determination kept everything running smoothly.

"Jack, we need those stabilizers here now," Sarah Jane called out, checking her list. "We're almost ready to integrate them."

Jack, communicating with a team of Torchwood operatives, nodded. "They're on their way. Just a few more minutes."

Back in the main lab, the Doctor and Major Carter completed the final connections on the Disruptor. The device hummed with a low, steady energy, its core glowing with a soft blue light.

"It's ready," Carter said, her voice filled with a mix of relief and anticipation. "We've integrated the Genesis Protocol with the Quantum Matrix Disruptor. Now we just need to connect it to the crystalline structure."

The team gathered around as the Doctor carefully positioned the Disruptor at the heart of the crystalline lattice. The air was thick with tension as he made the final adjustments.

"Everyone, stand back," the Doctor instructed. "I'm about to activate the weapon."

With a deep breath, he activated the device. The room filled with a brilliant light as the crystalline structure resonated with the energy from the Disruptor. The frequency modulation was perfect, the sound vibrating through the air like a harmonic symphony.

"It's working," Daniel Jackson said, his voice awed. "The crystals are amplifying the frequency exactly as described in the texts."

The Doctor, his face lit with triumph, nodded. "We've done it. This weapon will turn the Replicators' own technology against them. It's time to test it."

The team moved quickly, transporting the weapon to a secure testing area. The TARDIS materialized at a remote site where a controlled group of Replicators had been lured for the test.

"Everyone ready?" the Doctor asked, his hand poised over the activation switch.

"Ready," they replied in unison.

The Doctor activated the weapon, and a beam of pure, resonating energy shot out, enveloping the Replicators. The effect was immediate and dramatic. The Replicators convulsed as their molecular structure began to break down. The frequency, amplified by the crystalline structure, forced their replication process to turn inward, causing them to disassemble at a fundamental level.

"It's working!" Rose shouted, her face alight with excitement. "They're breaking apart!"

The Replicators, unable to adapt to the precise frequency, disintegrated into dust. The team watched in awe as the entire swarm was neutralized.

Colonel O'Neill clapped the Doctor on the back. "Nice work, Doc. This is the game-changer we needed."

Teal'c, his voice filled with quiet satisfaction, added, "The Replicators will not recover from this."

Sarah Jane, her eyes shining with relief, said, "We've finally found the key to defeating them."

Jack Harkness grinned broadly. "Let's take this weapon to the Replicators and finish this once and for all."

The Doctor, his hearts swelling with pride and determination, addressed his companions. "We've built a powerful weapon, but we still have work to do. The Replicators won't go down without a fight. But with this, we have a real chance to end their threat forever."

Kate Stewart's voice came over the comms, filled with relief and hope. "The weapon is a success. UNIT is ready to deploy it wherever necessary. We're with you all the way, Doctor."

With their spirits high and the ultimate weapon in hand, the team prepared for the final battle. The universe had never faced a threat like the Replicators, but with the Genesis Protocol and the Quantum Matrix Disruptor, they had the means to ensure victory.

As the TARDIS dematerialized, the Doctor addressed his companions one last time. "We've come a long way, and the end is in sight. Let's finish this and save the universe."

Rose, standing beside him, nodded. "To the end, Doctor."

With renewed resolve and the powerful weapon they had built together, the team set out for the ultimate showdown with the Replicators. The fight would be fierce, but they were ready to protect the universe from any threat, standing united until the very end.

Chapter 26: Testing the Weapon

The TARDIS materialized on a remote asteroid, far from any inhabited planets. The asteroid had been chosen as the testing ground for the newly built weapon, integrating the Genesis Protocol and the Quantum Matrix Disruptor. The atmosphere inside the TARDIS was tense, filled with anticipation and the weight of the task ahead.

The Doctor, Major Carter, and Daniel Jackson stood by the central console, reviewing the final schematics and ensuring the weapon was fully operational. Rose, Jack Harkness, Sarah Jane, and SG-1 were gathered around, ready to assist.

"We're ready to test the weapon," the Doctor announced, his voice steady. "We've lured a small group of Replicators to this asteroid. This will be our first field test."

Colonel O'Neill, ever the pragmatist, checked his weapon. "Let's hope this thing works. We've got one shot to get it right."

Major Carter adjusted the controls on the weapon, ensuring the frequency modulation was precise. "The calculations are solid. We just need to see how it performs in the field."

Teal'c, his expression stoic, stood ready with his staff weapon. "The Replicators are relentless. We must be prepared for any outcome."

The Doctor, with a nod to his companions, activated the external sensors. The viewscreen displayed the barren surface of the asteroid, dotted with metallic glints as the Replicators began to emerge from their hiding places.

"Everyone, to your positions," the Doctor instructed. "We'll deploy the weapon from here."

The team moved quickly, setting up the weapon outside the TARDIS. The crystalline structure and the Disruptor hummed with energy, the air crackling with the power contained within.

"Activating the Genesis Protocol," Major Carter said, her fingers moving deftly over the controls. "We're ready."

The Doctor took a deep breath and activated the weapon. A beam of pure energy shot out, enveloping the small group of Replicators. The

Replicators convulsed as the frequency began to disrupt their molecular structure.

"It's working," Rose said, her voice filled with hope. "They're starting to break apart."

But then, something unexpected happened. The Replicators, although initially affected, began to adapt. Their forms stabilized, and they started to reform, albeit more slowly and with apparent difficulty.

"Doctor, they're adapting!" Major Carter shouted, her voice tense. "We need to increase the power."

The Doctor adjusted the controls, pushing the weapon to its limits. The energy beam intensified, and the Replicators convulsed again, their forms breaking apart more violently this time. But they were still not completely destroyed.

"Come on, come on," the Doctor muttered, his eyes fixed on the viewscreen. "Just a little more."

Jack Harkness, seeing the Replicators struggling, added, "We need to keep the pressure on. Don't give them a chance to recover."

Teal'c fired his staff weapon, adding to the assault. "We must maintain the attack."

The Replicators began to falter, their adaptation processes overwhelmed by the combined assault. One by one, they started to disintegrate into dust. The air was filled with the sounds of their destruction, a chaotic symphony of victory.

"We're doing it," Sarah Jane said, her voice filled with relief. "They're falling apart."

But just as victory seemed within grasp, a new wave of Replicators emerged, larger and more resilient than before. They had adapted to the weapon's frequency and were now countering it more effectively.

"Doctor, we've got more incoming!" Daniel Jackson shouted, pointing to the viewscreen.

The Doctor's face hardened. "We need to recalibrate the frequency. Quickly, before they fully adapt."

Major Carter, working frantically, adjusted the controls. "I'm on it. Just a few more seconds."

The new wave of Replicators advanced, their forms shifting and adapting to the weapon's energy. The team fought valiantly, but the Replicators were learning and evolving.

"We can't let them get too close!" Rose shouted, firing her weapon.

Jack Harkness, grimly determined, added, "We've got to hold the line!"

The Doctor and Carter finally managed to recalibrate the frequency. The weapon pulsed with renewed energy, the beam shifting to a higher frequency. The Replicators, caught off guard by the change, convulsed violently and began to disintegrate.

"It's working again," Carter said, her voice filled with urgency. "But we need to keep changing the frequency to stay ahead of them."

The team continued to fight, adjusting the weapon's settings and keeping the Replicators off balance. Slowly but surely, the new wave began to falter and fall apart, their adaptations unable to keep up with the rapid changes in frequency.

As the last of the Replicators disintegrated, the team breathed a collective sigh of relief. The weapon had worked, but it was clear that the Replicators' ability to adapt posed a significant challenge.

"We did it," Rose said, her face alight with triumph. "But that was close."

Colonel O'Neill nodded, his expression serious. "Too close. We need to find a way to keep them from adapting so quickly."

Teal'c, his voice calm, added, "We have gained valuable insights from this test. We must refine the weapon further."

The Doctor, his face thoughtful, addressed the group. "We've made significant progress, but we're not there yet. The Replicators are incredibly resilient. We need to continue refining the weapon and find a way to stay ahead of their adaptations."

Major Carter agreed. "We need to build in a variable frequency modulator that can automatically adjust the frequency in real-time. That should make it harder for them to adapt."

Sarah Jane, ever the optimist, said, "We're getting closer. We just need to keep pushing."

Jack Harkness, with his trademark grin, added, "We'll get there. We've come too far to turn back now."

With renewed determination, the team returned to the TARDIS, ready to make the necessary adjustments to the weapon. They had faced a formidable challenge, but their resolve was stronger than ever. Together, they would refine the weapon and prepare for the final battle against the Replicators.

As the TARDIS dematerialized, the Doctor addressed his companions one last time. "We've come a long way, and the end is in sight. Let's finish this and save the universe."

Rose, standing beside him, nodded. "To the end, Doctor."

With their spirits high and their resolve unwavering, the team set out for the ultimate showdown with the Replicators. The fight would be fierce, but they were ready to protect the universe from any threat, standing united until the very end.

Chapter 27: Replicator Adaptation

The TARDIS hummed with a renewed sense of urgency as it materialized in the heart of the UNIT command center. The successful, yet troubling test of the new weapon had given the team insight into the Replicators' adaptability. Now, they had to refine the weapon to stay ahead of the relentless enemy.

The Doctor, Major Carter, and Daniel Jackson stood by the central console, deep in discussion. Rose, Jack Harkness, Sarah Jane, and SG-1 were gathered around, ready to assist in any way they could.

"That last test showed us that the Replicators can adapt faster than we anticipated," the Doctor began, his voice tense but determined. "We need to stay ahead of their adaptations if we're going to stand a chance."

Major Carter nodded, her eyes focused on the schematics spread out before them. "We need to build a variable frequency modulator into the weapon. It has to automatically adjust the frequency in real-time to stay effective."

Daniel Jackson added, "The ancient texts mentioned a secondary failsafe mechanism. If we can integrate that, it might give us an extra layer of protection."

Colonel O'Neill, always pragmatic, looked at the group. "Let's get to it. We don't have much time before the Replicators adapt again."

Teal'c, standing guard as always, added, "We must act swiftly. The Replicators will not wait."

The team split into smaller groups, each tasked with refining different aspects of the weapon. The Doctor and Major Carter focused on integrating the variable frequency modulator, while Daniel Jackson and Sarah Jane worked on deciphering the failsafe mechanism from the ancient texts. Rose, Jack Harkness, and SG-1 coordinated the logistics and managed the influx of necessary components.

In the secure lab, Major Carter and the Doctor worked side by side, their hands moving swiftly over the intricate circuitry of the Disruptor.

The room buzzed with the sound of welding, the hum of machinery, and the low murmur of intense concentration.

"We need to ensure the frequency modulator can adjust in real-time," Carter explained, adjusting the controls. "Even the slightest delay could give the Replicators enough time to adapt."

The Doctor nodded, using his sonic screwdriver to fine-tune the connections. "The TARDIS's systems should help us achieve the necessary precision. We can link the modulator to the TARDIS's temporal matrix for instantaneous adjustments."

Daniel Jackson, translating a particularly complex section of the ancient texts, added, "The failsafe mechanism involves creating a feedback loop within the Replicators' own systems. It's designed to overload their adaptive algorithms."

Sarah Jane, ever resourceful, worked on integrating the failsafe mechanism. "We can tie this into the weapon's main system. It will trigger automatically if the primary frequency fails."

Rose and Jack, coordinating the logistics, ensured that each component arrived on time and in perfect condition. The logistics were a monumental task, but their experience and determination kept everything running smoothly.

"Jack, we need those stabilizers here now," Rose called out, checking her list. "We're almost ready to integrate them."

Jack, communicating with a team of Torchwood operatives, nodded. "They're on their way. Just a few more minutes."

As the assembly progressed, the team's determination grew stronger. They knew the stakes and were ready to face the challenge head-on.

Back in the main lab, the Doctor and Major Carter completed the final connections on the Disruptor. The device hummed with a low, steady energy, its core glowing with a soft blue light.

"It's ready," Carter said, her voice filled with a mix of relief and anticipation. "We've integrated the variable frequency modulator and the failsafe mechanism."

The Doctor nodded, his face resolute. "Then it's time to test it again. Let's save the universe."

The TARDIS materialized at a remote testing site, where a controlled group of Replicators had been lured for the test. The atmosphere was tense as the team prepared to deploy the refined weapon.

"Everyone ready?" the Doctor asked, his hand poised over the activation switch.

"Ready," they replied in unison.

The Doctor activated the weapon. A beam of pure, resonating energy shot out, enveloping the Replicators. At first, the Replicators convulsed as the frequency began to disrupt their molecular structure. However, this time, the variable frequency modulator kicked in, constantly adjusting the frequency to stay ahead of the Replicators' adaptations.

"It's working," Rose said, her voice filled with hope. "They're starting to break apart."

But then, something unexpected happened. The Replicators, although initially affected, began to adapt again. Their forms stabilized, and they started to reform, albeit more slowly and with apparent difficulty.

"Doctor, they're adapting again!" Major Carter shouted, her voice tense. "We need to increase the power."

The Doctor adjusted the controls, pushing the weapon to its limits. The energy beam intensified, and the Replicators convulsed again, their forms breaking apart more violently this time. But they were still not completely destroyed.

"Come on, come on," the Doctor muttered, his eyes fixed on the viewscreen. "Just a little more."

Jack Harkness, seeing the Replicators struggling, added, "We need to keep the pressure on. Don't give them a chance to recover."

Teal'c fired his staff weapon, adding to the assault. "We must maintain the attack."

The Replicators began to falter, their adaptation processes overwhelmed by the combined assault. One by one, they started to disintegrate into dust. The air was filled with the sounds of their destruction, a chaotic symphony of victory.

"We're doing it," Sarah Jane said, her voice filled with relief. "They're falling apart."

But just as victory seemed within grasp, a new wave of Replicators emerged, larger and more resilient than before. They had adapted to the weapon's frequency and were now countering it more effectively.

"Doctor, we've got more incoming!" Daniel Jackson shouted, pointing to the viewscreen.

The Doctor's face hardened. "We need to recalibrate the frequency. Quickly, before they fully adapt."

Major Carter, working frantically, adjusted the controls. "I'm on it. Just a few more seconds."

The new wave of Replicators advanced, their forms shifting and adapting to the weapon's energy. The team fought valiantly, but the Replicators were learning and evolving.

"We can't let them get too close!" Rose shouted, firing her weapon.

Jack Harkness, grimly determined, added, "We've got to hold the line!"

The Doctor and Carter finally managed to recalibrate the frequency. The weapon pulsed with renewed energy, the beam shifting to a higher frequency. The Replicators, caught off guard by the change, convulsed violently and began to disintegrate.

"It's working again," Carter said, her voice filled with urgency. "But we need to keep changing the frequency to stay ahead of them."

The team continued to fight, adjusting the weapon's settings and keeping the Replicators off balance. Slowly but surely, the new wave began to falter and fall apart, their adaptations unable to keep up with the rapid changes in frequency.

As the last of the Replicators disintegrated, the team breathed a collective sigh of relief. The weapon had worked, but it was clear that the Replicators' ability to adapt posed a significant challenge.

"We did it," Rose said, her face alight with triumph. "But that was close."

Colonel O'Neill nodded, his expression serious. "Too close. We need to find a way to keep them from adapting so quickly."

Teal'c, his voice calm, added, "We have gained valuable insights from this test. We must refine the weapon further."

The Doctor, his face thoughtful, addressed the group. "We've made significant progress, but we're not there yet. The Replicators are incredibly resilient. We need to continue refining the weapon and find a way to stay ahead of their adaptations."

Major Carter agreed. "We need to build in a variable frequency modulator that can automatically adjust the frequency in real-time. That should make it harder for them to adapt."

Sarah Jane, ever the optimist, said, "We're getting closer. We just need to keep pushing."

Jack Harkness, with his trademark grin, added, "We'll get there. We've come too far to turn back now."

With renewed determination, the team returned to the TARDIS, ready to make the necessary adjustments to the weapon. They had faced a formidable challenge, but their resolve was stronger than ever. Together, they would refine the weapon and prepare for the final battle against the Replicators.

As the TARDIS dematerialized, the Doctor addressed his companions one last time. "We've come a long way, and the end is in sight. Let's finish this and save the universe."

Rose, standing beside him, nodded. "To the end, Doctor."

With their spirits high and their resolve unwavering, the team set out for the ultimate showdown with the Replicators. The fight would be fierce, but they were ready to protect the universe from any threat, standing united until the very end.

Chapter 28: Torchwood's Secret

The TARDIS materialized with its familiar wheeze and thud in the heart of Cardiff, right outside the iconic Torchwood Hub. The recent battle against the Replicators had left the team searching for any advantage they could find. Jack Harkness had hinted at a secret stash of alien artifacts hidden within Torchwood that might provide the edge they needed.

As the team exited the TARDIS, Jack turned to the Doctor, his eyes serious but hopeful. "Doctor, there's something I haven't told you. Torchwood has been collecting alien artifacts for years. We've got a hidden vault full of things that might just help us against the Replicators."

The Doctor raised an eyebrow, intrigued. "You've been holding out on us, Jack. This better be good."

Jack led the way through the Hub, past the familiar workstations and equipment, to a secure door at the back of the facility. He placed his hand on a biometric scanner, and the door slid open with a hiss, revealing a dimly lit staircase descending into the depths of Torchwood.

"Welcome to Torchwood's Vault," Jack said, his voice echoing off the stone walls. "We've been collecting these artifacts for years, just in case we ever needed them."

The team followed Jack down the staircase and into a vast underground chamber filled with shelves and display cases, each one holding a different piece of alien technology. The air was thick with the hum of energy and the faint glow of various devices.

Rose's eyes widened as she took in the sight. "Jack, this is incredible. Why didn't you tell us about this sooner?"

Jack shrugged, a sly grin on his face. "Didn't think we needed it until now. Besides, some of these artifacts are pretty dangerous."

Sarah Jane moved closer to one of the shelves, examining a crystalline structure that pulsed with a soft blue light. "What do we have here, Jack?"

Jack joined her, picking up the crystal carefully. "This is a Psion Crystal. It's capable of amplifying psychic energy. Could be useful for boosting our weapon's power."

Major Carter, her scientific curiosity piqued, asked, "What else do you have? Anything related to energy manipulation or frequency modulation?"

Jack led them to another section of the vault, where several spherical devices rested on pedestals. "These are Radion Spheres. They can emit high-frequency energy bursts. We might be able to integrate them with our current weapon to enhance its effectiveness."

Teal'c, ever vigilant, examined a set of metallic rods with intricate carvings. "What are these, Captain Harkness?"

Jack's grin widened. "Ah, those are Zeta Rods. They generate a powerful electromagnetic field. Could be used to disrupt the Replicators' molecular cohesion."

The Doctor, his mind racing with possibilities, turned to Jack. "We'll need to integrate these artifacts with the TARDIS's systems and our existing weapon. It'll be tricky, but with these, we might just have a fighting chance."

The team got to work, carefully transporting the artifacts back to the TARDIS. The atmosphere was electric with anticipation as they prepared to integrate the new technology. Major Carter and the Doctor took the lead, their hands moving deftly over the intricate circuitry and controls.

"Let's start with the Psion Crystal," Carter suggested. "We can use it to boost the power output of the Quantum Matrix Disruptor."

The Doctor nodded, his sonic screwdriver buzzing as he made the necessary adjustments. "The crystal's energy can be channeled through the TARDIS's power grid, amplifying the Disruptor's frequency."

Daniel Jackson, working with Sarah Jane, examined the Radion Spheres. "We can integrate these spheres to emit synchronized energy bursts, creating a more powerful and disruptive frequency."

Sarah Jane nodded, her face set with determination. "I'll help with the connections. We need to make sure everything is perfectly aligned."

Rose and Jack handled the Zeta Rods, carefully positioning them around the central console. "These rods will generate an electromagnetic field that can destabilize the Replicators," Jack explained. "We'll need to synchronize them with the Disruptor's output."

As the final adjustments were made, the TARDIS hummed with a new, powerful energy. The Doctor stepped back, admiring their work. "We've integrated Torchwood's artifacts with the Quantum Matrix Disruptor. This weapon is now more powerful than ever."

Colonel O'Neill, always ready for action, asked, "Where do we test it?"

The Doctor's eyes gleamed with determination. "There's a known Replicator stronghold on a distant moon. It's heavily fortified, but with this weapon, we have a real chance to take them down."

The TARDIS materialized on the surface of the moon, the harsh landscape illuminated by the eerie glow of the Replicator stronghold. The team moved quickly, setting up the weapon and preparing for the test.

"Everyone ready?" the Doctor asked, his hand poised over the activation switch.

"Ready," they replied in unison.

The Doctor activated the weapon. A beam of pure, resonating energy shot out, enveloping the Replicator stronghold. The Psion Crystal amplified the power, while the Radion Spheres emitted synchronized energy bursts. The Zeta Rods generated a powerful electromagnetic field, destabilizing the Replicators' molecular cohesion.

The Replicators convulsed, their forms breaking apart as the weapon's enhanced frequency disrupted their structure. The air was filled with the sounds of their disintegration, a chaotic symphony of victory.

"It's working," Rose said, her voice filled with hope. "They're falling apart."

But then, something unexpected happened. The Replicators began to adapt once again, their forms stabilizing and starting to reform. However, the integration of Torchwood's artifacts gave the weapon an edge. The Psion Crystal and Radion Spheres created a feedback loop, continuously adjusting the frequency and keeping the Replicators off balance.

"We need to keep the pressure on," Major Carter shouted. "Don't let them recover!"

Teal'c fired his staff weapon, adding to the assault. "We must maintain the attack."

The Doctor, making rapid adjustments to the controls, increased the power output. "Come on, just a little more."

The Replicators began to falter, their adaptations overwhelmed by the continuous feedback loop. One by one, they started to disintegrate into dust. The air was filled with the sounds of their destruction, a chaotic symphony of victory.

"We're doing it," Sarah Jane said, her voice filled with relief. "They're falling apart."

As the last of the Replicators disintegrated, the team breathed a collective sigh of relief. The weapon had worked, and the integration of Torchwood's artifacts had given them the edge they needed.

"We did it," Rose said, her face alight with triumph. "That was close."

Colonel O'Neill nodded, his expression serious. "Too close. But we've got a fighting chance now."

Teal'c, his voice calm, added, "This is a significant victory. We must remain vigilant."

Jack Harkness grinned broadly. "Torchwood's secret stash came through. Let's take this weapon to the Replicators and finish this once and for all."

The Doctor, his hearts swelling with pride and determination, addressed his companions. "We've built a powerful weapon, but we still have work to do. The Replicators won't go down without a fight. But with this, we have a real chance to end their threat forever."

With renewed hope and the powerful weapon in hand, the team prepared for the final battle. The universe had never faced a threat like the Replicators, but with the Genesis Protocol, the Quantum Matrix Disruptor, and Torchwood's artifacts, they had the means to ensure victory.

As the TARDIS dematerialized, the Doctor addressed his companions one last time. "We've come a long way, and the end is in sight. Let's finish this and save the universe."

Rose, standing beside him, nodded. "To the end, Doctor."

With their spirits high and their resolve unwavering, the team set out for the ultimate showdown with the Replicators. The fight would be fierce, but they were ready to protect the universe from any threat, standing united until the very end.

Chapter 29: UNIT's Last Stand

The air was thick with tension as the TARDIS materialized in the heart of the UNIT command center. The recent successes had given the team hope, but the Replicators' relentless advance showed no signs of slowing. With the final battle looming, UNIT was preparing for a last-ditch effort to hold off the Replicators and buy the Doctor and his allies the time they needed to enact their final plan.

Kate Stewart, her face set with determination, addressed the assembled troops. "This is it, everyone. The Replicators are closing in, and we need to hold them off at all costs. This is our last stand."

The Doctor, standing beside her, nodded. "We've made incredible progress, but we need more time to implement the final plan. UNIT will hold the line while we prepare."

Major Carter, Daniel Jackson, Teal'c, Colonel O'Neill, Sarah Jane, Rose, and Jack Harkness were gathered around the central table, poring over the final schematics and strategies. The atmosphere was a mix of urgency and resolve.

"We've integrated the artifacts and refined the weapon," Carter explained. "But we need to set up a larger-scale deployment. We'll need to use the TARDIS and the Odyssey to amplify the signal across the entire planet."

Colonel O'Neill looked at the Doctor. "We're counting on you to get that signal ready. We'll hold off the Replicators as long as we can."

Teal'c, his voice calm and steady, added, "We must act swiftly. The Replicators will not delay their assault."

Jack Harkness, always ready for action, grinned. "Let's give them hell."

The Doctor turned to Kate. "UNIT's defenses are strong, but the Replicators are relentless. We'll need every available resource to hold them off."

Kate nodded. "We're ready, Doctor. UNIT is prepared to fight to the last man."

As the team moved to their positions, the Doctor and Major Carter began the final preparations for the planetary defense. The TARDIS and the Odyssey would work in tandem to deploy the amplified signal, creating a protective barrier and a powerful weapon against the Replicators.

"Rose, Sarah Jane, Jack, I need you to assist with the TARDIS controls," the Doctor instructed. "Carter, you'll handle the coordination with the Odyssey."

Colonel O'Neill, Teal'c, and Daniel Jackson joined Kate Stewart and the UNIT soldiers on the front lines. The air was filled with the hum of energy weapons and the distant sound of Replicator clattering.

"We've got incoming!" a UNIT officer shouted, pointing to the horizon.

The first wave of Replicators appeared, a shimmering mass of metallic bodies moving with terrifying precision. The ground shook as they advanced, their eyes glowing with malevolent intent.

"Hold the line!" Kate commanded, her voice unwavering. "Do not let them breach our defenses!"

The battle erupted in a cacophony of sound and fury. UNIT soldiers and SG-1 fired their weapons, the air filled with the sharp crack of energy rifles and the deep thrum of Teal'c's staff weapon. The Replicators surged forward, their bodies shattering under the assault but reforming almost instantly.

"We need more firepower!" Colonel O'Neill shouted, his P90 rattling off rounds. "Keep them off balance!"

Teal'c moved with precision, his staff weapon blazing as he targeted the Replicators' weak points. "We must not let them advance."

Daniel Jackson, using a portable energy weapon, provided cover fire. "We're holding them, but we need that signal up and running!"

Back in the TARDIS, the Doctor and Major Carter worked frantically to synchronize the systems. "We need to amplify the signal and ensure it's stable," Carter said, her hands moving over the controls.

The Doctor nodded, his sonic screwdriver buzzing as he made adjustments. "The TARDIS's temporal matrix should help stabilize the signal. We just need to align it with the Odyssey's systems."

Rose, monitoring the power levels, called out, "We're at 75% capacity. Almost there!"

Sarah Jane and Jack worked on integrating the Radion Spheres and Zeta Rods into the TARDIS's systems. "These artifacts should give us the edge we need," Jack said, connecting the last of the Zeta Rods.

"We're ready," Sarah Jane confirmed. "Let's activate the signal."

With a final nod from the Doctor, Major Carter activated the system. The TARDIS and the Odyssey hummed with a powerful energy, the signal amplifying and spreading across the planet.

Outside, the Replicators convulsed as the signal hit them, their forms destabilizing. The synchronized energy bursts from the Radion Spheres and the electromagnetic field from the Zeta Rods created a devastating effect.

"It's working!" Carter shouted, monitoring the readings. "The signal is holding!"

The Replicators, caught in the feedback loop, began to disintegrate en masse. The air was filled with the sound of their destruction, a chaotic symphony of victory.

"We're doing it," Rose said, her face alight with triumph. "They're falling apart."

But then, a new wave of Replicators emerged, larger and more resilient than before. They had adapted to the signal and were now countering it more effectively.

"Doctor, we've got more incoming!" Daniel Jackson shouted, pointing to the viewscreen.

The Doctor's face hardened. "We need to recalibrate the frequency. Quickly, before they fully adapt."

Major Carter, working frantically, adjusted the controls. "I'm on it. Just a few more seconds."

The new wave of Replicators advanced, their forms shifting and adapting to the signal. The team fought valiantly, but the Replicators were learning and evolving.

"We can't let them get too close!" Rose shouted, firing her weapon.

Jack Harkness, grimly determined, added, "We've got to hold the line!"

The Doctor and Carter finally managed to recalibrate the frequency. The signal pulsed with renewed energy, the beam shifting to a higher frequency. The Replicators, caught off guard by the change, convulsed violently and began to disintegrate.

"It's working again," Carter said, her voice filled with urgency. "But we need to keep changing the frequency to stay ahead of them."

The team continued to fight, adjusting the weapon's settings and keeping the Replicators off balance. Slowly but surely, the new wave began to falter and fall apart, their adaptations unable to keep up with the rapid changes in frequency.

As the last of the Replicators disintegrated, the team breathed a collective sigh of relief. The weapon had worked, and the integration of Torchwood's artifacts had given them the edge they needed.

"We did it," Rose said, her face alight with triumph. "But that was close."

Colonel O'Neill nodded, his expression serious. "Too close. But we've got a fighting chance now."

Teal'c, his voice calm, added, "This is a significant victory. We must remain vigilant."

Jack Harkness grinned broadly. "Torchwood's secret stash came through. Let's take this weapon to the Replicators and finish this once and for all."

The Doctor, his hearts swelling with pride and determination, addressed his companions. "We've built a powerful weapon, but we still have work to do. The Replicators won't go down without a fight. But with this, we have a real chance to end their threat forever."

With renewed hope and the powerful weapon in hand, the team prepared for the final battle. The universe had never faced a threat like the Replicators, but with the Genesis Protocol, the Quantum Matrix Disruptor, and Torchwood's artifacts, they had the means to ensure victory.

As the TARDIS dematerialized, the Doctor addressed his companions one last time. "We've come a long way, and the end is in sight. Let's finish this and save the universe."

Rose, standing beside him, nodded. "To the end, Doctor."

With their spirits high and their resolve unwavering, the team set out for the ultimate showdown with the Replicators. The fight would be fierce, but they were ready to protect the universe from any threat, standing united until the very end.

Chapter 30: The Doctor's Revelation

The TARDIS hummed quietly, an oasis of calm amid the chaos of battle preparations. The Doctor paced the console room, his brow furrowed in deep thought. The recent battles had given them hope but also revealed the true tenacity of the Replicators. As his companions worked on refining their weapons and strategies, the Doctor pondered over every detail they had uncovered about the Replicators.

"Doctor, are you alright?" Rose asked, her voice tinged with concern. She and the rest of the team had noticed his growing intensity.

The Doctor stopped pacing and looked at her, his eyes bright with a sudden realization. "Rose, I think I've been looking at this all wrong. The Replicators... they're not just machines. They're a form of life. And like all life, they have a core drive, a central purpose. If we can understand that, we can stop them."

Colonel O'Neill, standing nearby with his arms crossed, raised an eyebrow. "You mean like a hive mind? We've dealt with those before."

The Doctor shook his head. "Not exactly. The Replicators are more complex. They're driven by a fundamental directive to evolve and survive. But what if we could disrupt that directive?"

Major Carter, intrigued, stepped closer. "How do we do that, Doctor? We've tried everything to disrupt their programming."

The Doctor's eyes gleamed with excitement. "We've been focusing on their physical forms and their ability to adapt. But what if we target their core programming—the very essence of their drive to replicate and adapt?"

Teal'c, ever the warrior, asked, "How do you propose we achieve this, Doctor?"

The Doctor turned to the central console and began typing furiously. "The key lies in their communication network. The Replicators share information through a complex network of signals. If we can insert a signal into that network, one that disrupts their core directive, we can stop them from adapting."

Daniel Jackson, his mind racing with possibilities, added, "You mean like a virus? Something that spreads through their network and corrupts their programming?"

The Doctor nodded. "Exactly. But it needs to be more than just a simple virus. It has to be a fundamental disruption—a revelation that causes their entire system to collapse."

Jack Harkness grinned. "I like the sound of that. How do we create this... revelation?"

The Doctor continued typing, pulling up schematics and data on the viewscreen. "We use the Genesis Protocol and the Quantum Matrix Disruptor to create a signal, but we embed it with a self-replicating algorithm. This algorithm will spread through their network, targeting the core directive and causing a cascading failure."

Sarah Jane, her eyes wide with understanding, said, "But we need to ensure that the signal is strong enough to reach every part of their network."

The Doctor smiled. "That's where the TARDIS and the Odyssey come in. We use both to amplify the signal and spread it across the entire planet—no, the entire galaxy if we need to."

Major Carter's face lit up with excitement. "We can use the Asgard technology on the Odyssey to boost the signal. It's risky, but it could work."

Colonel O'Neill nodded. "Then let's get to it. We don't have much time."

The team sprang into action, each member taking on their assigned tasks. Major Carter and the Doctor worked on creating the self-replicating algorithm, while Daniel Jackson and Sarah Jane prepared the signal matrix. Teal'c and Colonel O'Neill coordinated the defenses with UNIT, ensuring they could hold off the Replicators long enough for the plan to work.

Rose and Jack Harkness assisted with the integration of the TARDIS and Odyssey systems, ensuring that the signal could be amplified to its maximum potential.

As they worked, the tension in the air was palpable. They knew this was their last chance to stop the Replicators once and for all.

"Doctor, the algorithm is ready," Carter said, handing him a data crystal. "We just need to integrate it into the signal matrix."

The Doctor took the crystal and inserted it into the console. "Let's hope this works."

With the final adjustments made, the TARDIS and Odyssey were synchronized, ready to broadcast the disruptive signal.

"Everyone, to your positions," the Doctor commanded. "We're about to change the course of this war."

The TARDIS and Odyssey began to hum with an intense energy, the signal building to a crescendo. The Doctor activated the system, and a beam of pure, resonating energy shot out, carrying the self-replicating algorithm.

The signal spread across the planet, reaching every Replicator in its path. At first, nothing seemed to happen. Then, one by one, the Replicators began to convulse. Their forms destabilized, and a chaotic disarray spread through their network.

"It's working," Rose said, her voice filled with hope. "They're breaking apart."

The Replicators, unable to adapt to the new algorithm, began to disintegrate en masse. Their network collapsed, and their core directive was disrupted beyond repair.

Colonel O'Neill watched in awe. "Doc, you did it. They're falling apart."

Teal'c, ever calm, added, "The Replicators are defeated. We have succeeded."

As the last of the Replicators disintegrated, the team breathed a collective sigh of relief. The battle was over, and they had won.

The Doctor, his face reflecting a mix of exhaustion and triumph, addressed his companions. "We've done it. The Replicators are no more."

Sarah Jane, tears of relief in her eyes, said, "You saved us, Doctor. You saved everyone."

Jack Harkness grinned. "I knew you'd figure it out, Doc. We couldn't have done it without you."

Rose, standing beside the Doctor, hugged him tightly. "To the end, Doctor."

The Doctor smiled, his hearts swelling with pride and gratitude. "To the end, Rose."

With the Replicator threat finally over, the team knew they had achieved something extraordinary. They had faced impossible odds and emerged victorious, united in their determination to protect the universe.

As the TARDIS dematerialized, the Doctor reflected on the journey they had taken. They had come together from different worlds, different times, and had stood united against a common enemy. And in the end, it was their unity, their courage, and their unyielding spirit that had saved the universe.

With their spirits high and their resolve unwavering, the team looked forward to whatever new adventures awaited them, ready to face any challenge and protect the universe from any threat, standing united until the very end.

Chapter 31: Coordinated Strike

The TARDIS materialized on a secure military base, its surroundings buzzing with activity. UNIT, Torchwood, and the combined forces of SG-1 were in a frenzy of preparation. The final, coordinated strike against the Replicators was about to commence. The Replicators, though weakened by the Doctor's revelation, still posed a significant threat, and this strike was meant to be the decisive blow.

The Doctor, Major Carter, Daniel Jackson, Teal'c, Colonel O'Neill, Sarah Jane, Rose, and Jack Harkness were gathered around a large holographic display table in the command center. Kate Stewart, the head of UNIT, was briefing the team.

"Alright, everyone, this is it," Kate began, her voice firm and clear. "The Replicators are regrouping, but we have a narrow window to strike before they can fully adapt to the disruption algorithm. This coordinated strike is our best chance to wipe them out for good."

The holographic display showed the strategic points where the Replicators had established strongholds. The plan was to hit these points simultaneously, using the upgraded weapon with the Genesis Protocol, enhanced by Torchwood's artifacts.

Colonel O'Neill took the lead in coordinating the assault. "We'll divide into three teams. SG-1 and UNIT will hit the primary stronghold here," he pointed to a large red marker on the map. "Torchwood and the Doctor will target this secondary location. The third team, led by Kate and reinforced with Asgard technology from the Odyssey, will attack this position."

Teal'c, standing beside O'Neill, added, "Our combined forces must strike with precision. We cannot allow the Replicators to adapt to our tactics."

Jack Harkness grinned, his confidence unshaken. "Let's show them what we're made of."

The Doctor, adjusting his sonic screwdriver, looked at the team with determination. "Remember, the key is to keep the pressure on and adapt faster than they can. We've got the technology and the strategy. Now we just need to execute."

As the teams moved out, the atmosphere was charged with anticipation and resolve. The assault vehicles, heavily armored and equipped with the latest technology, rolled out of the base. The air was filled with the hum of engines and the clatter of weapons being checked one last time.

Team One: SG-1 and UNIT

Colonel O'Neill, Major Carter, Daniel Jackson, and Teal'c led the first team. Their target was the largest Replicator stronghold. As they approached, the ground shook with the presence of the Replicators, their metallic forms glinting in the harsh light.

"Engage on my mark," O'Neill commanded. "Three, two, one—mark!"

The soldiers opened fire, energy weapons blazing. The Replicators responded with a furious assault, but the upgraded weapons, powered by the Genesis Protocol, began to destabilize their forms.

"Keep pushing forward!" Major Carter shouted, her voice cutting through the chaos. "We need to reach the central core!"

Teal'c, his staff weapon blazing, moved with precision, taking down Replicators with each shot. "We must not let them regroup."

Daniel Jackson, using a portable energy device, targeted the Replicators' communication nodes. "Disrupt their network. It's their weakest point!"

Team Two: Torchwood and the Doctor

The Doctor, Rose, Jack Harkness, and the Torchwood team approached their target location, a heavily fortified Replicator outpost. The TARDIS had been set up as a mobile command center, enhancing their ability to adapt and respond in real-time.

"Activate the disruptor," the Doctor ordered, his hands flying over the TARDIS console. "We need to create an opening."

The beam of energy shot out from the TARDIS, hitting the Replicators with a powerful burst. The Psion Crystal and Radion Spheres integrated into the weapon created a devastating effect, causing the Replicators to convulse and disintegrate.

Jack Harkness, leading the charge, grinned. "Alright, let's move! Keep them on the back foot!"

Rose, firing her weapon, added, "We need to reach their command node and plant the signal disruptor."

The Torchwood team moved with practiced efficiency, covering each other as they advanced. The Doctor, using his sonic screwdriver, disabled the Replicators' defenses, creating a clear path to their objective.

Team Three: Kate Stewart and Reinforced UNIT

Kate Stewart, leading the third team with the support of Asgard technology, targeted a critical Replicator installation. The Odyssey hovered above, ready to provide air support.

"Deploy the Asgard disruptors," Kate ordered. "We need to hit them hard and fast."

The ground forces advanced, their weapons powered by Asgard technology. The Replicators, caught off guard by the advanced weaponry, began to falter.

"Maintain formation!" Kate shouted. "Don't let them regroup!"

The combined firepower from the ground and the Odyssey's aerial assault created a devastating effect. The Replicators' defenses crumbled under the relentless assault.

Climax: Convergence

As each team advanced, the battle reached a fever pitch. The Replicators, struggling to adapt to the multi-pronged attack, began to show signs of disarray.

"Doctor, we're nearing the command node," Rose reported. "What's next?"

The Doctor, his mind racing, replied, "We need to plant the signal disruptor and synchronize it with the TARDIS and the Odyssey. It will send a cascading failure through their network."

"Almost there," Jack shouted, firing at the last line of Replicators guarding the node. "Cover me!"

Rose and the Torchwood team provided cover as Jack reached the node and planted the device. "Disruptor planted!"

"Activate it," the Doctor ordered. "Now!"

Jack activated the disruptor, and the signal spread through the Replicators' network. The effect was immediate and catastrophic. The Replicators convulsed, their forms breaking apart as the signal disrupted their core programming.

Victory: The Aftermath

As the last of the Replicators disintegrated, the battlefield fell silent. The combined forces had succeeded in their coordinated strike, dealing a decisive blow to the Replicators.

"We did it," Rose said, her voice filled with relief. "It's over."

Colonel O'Neill, surveying the battlefield, nodded. "Good job, everyone. We held the line."

Teal'c, ever stoic, added, "The Replicators are defeated. We have won."

Jack Harkness, grinning broadly, said, "That was one for the history books."

The Doctor, his hearts swelling with pride and gratitude, addressed his companions. "We faced impossible odds and emerged victorious. We did it together, as a team. The universe is safe because of all of you."

Kate Stewart, her face reflecting the weariness of battle but also immense pride, nodded. "UNIT, Torchwood, SG-1, and the Doctor's team—together, we achieved the impossible."

As the team regrouped and began to tend to the wounded and repair the damage, there was a sense of unity and triumph. They had faced a formidable enemy and won, standing together against the odds.

With the Replicator threat finally eliminated, the universe was safe once more. The Doctor and his companions knew that there would always be new challenges and adventures ahead, but they were ready to face them together.

As the TARDIS dematerialized, the Doctor looked at his friends, his eyes filled with hope. "Onward, to new adventures."

Rose, standing beside him, smiled. "To the end, Doctor."

With their spirits high and their resolve unwavering, the team looked forward to the future, ready to protect the universe from any threat, standing united until the very end.

Chapter 32: Unexpected Allies

The battlefield was still as the dust settled from the recent coordinated strike. The combined forces of UNIT, Torchwood, and SG-1 had dealt a crippling blow to the Replicators, but the atmosphere remained tense. The Replicators were relentless, and their ability to adapt made it clear that this victory, while significant, was not yet final.

The Doctor, Rose, Jack Harkness, Sarah Jane, and the members of SG-1 gathered in the TARDIS to assess their next move. The holographic display in the command center flickered with various readings, showing the weakened but still present Replicator activity.

"We've done a lot of damage, but it's not over," the Doctor said, his voice filled with determination. "We need to prepare for their next move."

Colonel O'Neill, standing with his arms crossed, nodded. "We've hit them hard, but they always come back. What's our next play?"

Before anyone could respond, the TARDIS console emitted a series of rapid beeps. The Doctor moved quickly to the controls, his eyes widening as he read the data.

"We're receiving a transmission," the Doctor announced. "It's... it's the Asgard."

The room fell silent as everyone absorbed the unexpected news. The Asgard, thought to be extinct after their mass suicide to avoid further degradation of their species, had somehow reached out.

"Put it through," Major Carter said, her voice tinged with hope and curiosity.

The holographic display flickered, and the image of an Asgard appeared. It was Thor, the Supreme Commander of the Asgard fleet, a familiar face to the SG-1 team.

"Greetings, Doctor," Thor said in his calm, measured tone. "And greetings to the combined forces of UNIT, Torchwood, and SG-1. We have detected your struggle against the Replicators and have come to offer our assistance."

"Thor!" Carter exclaimed, her face lighting up with relief and excitement. "We thought you were gone."

"Our physical forms may be gone, but our consciousnesses were preserved within a digital matrix," Thor explained. "We have continued to observe and, when necessary, intervene."

The Doctor stepped forward, his eyes filled with respect and gratitude. "Thor, your timing couldn't be better. We've dealt a significant blow to the Replicators, but we need every advantage we can get to finish this fight."

"Indeed," Thor replied. "We have developed a new weapon designed specifically to combat the adaptive capabilities of the Replicators. It is an enhancement of the technology you have already employed, integrating advanced Asgard energy modulation techniques."

Jack Harkness, ever the pragmatist, asked, "How do we deploy this new weapon?"

Thor's image flickered as he transmitted the schematics. "We will transfer the necessary components to your vessel. You must integrate them with your existing systems. This will amplify the Genesis Protocol and the Quantum Matrix Disruptor to a level that the Replicators cannot counter."

The Doctor nodded, already formulating a plan. "We'll need to work quickly. The Replicators won't give us much time."

The TARDIS materialized aboard the Asgard vessel, a sleek, technologically advanced ship hovering above the battlefield. The team moved quickly, guided by Thor's instructions, to integrate the new Asgard components with their existing weaponry.

Major Carter and the Doctor worked side by side, their hands moving swiftly over the intricate circuitry. "These components will allow us to modulate the frequency in real-time," Carter explained. "The Replicators won't be able to adapt."

The Doctor adjusted the settings with his sonic screwdriver. "And with the Asgard's energy modulation techniques, the signal will be powerful enough to reach every part of their network."

As they worked, Teal'c and Colonel O'Neill coordinated with the ground forces, preparing for the final assault. "We need to keep them off us long enough for the Doctor and Carter to finish the integration," O'Neill said. "Hold the line at all costs."

The combined forces took their positions, the air filled with the hum of engines and the clatter of weapons being prepared. The Replicators, sensing the renewed threat, began to regroup for a counterattack.

"Thor, we're ready," the Doctor announced, stepping back from the console. "Let's deploy the weapon."

Thor's image nodded. "The Asgard will provide cover from orbit. Good luck, Doctor. The fate of many worlds rests on your success."

The TARDIS and the Asgard vessel coordinated their systems, and a beam of pure, resonating energy shot out, enveloping the Replicator strongholds. The advanced energy modulation created by the Asgard components caused the Replicators to convulse, their forms breaking apart as the signal disrupted their core programming.

"It's working!" Rose shouted, her face alight with triumph. "They're disintegrating!"

But the Replicators, ever resilient, began to adapt. However, the Asgard's technology anticipated their adaptations, adjusting the frequency in real-time and overwhelming their ability to counter the signal.

"Keep the pressure on!" Major Carter commanded. "We're almost there!"

The combined forces of UNIT, Torchwood, and SG-1 launched their assault with renewed vigor. The Replicators, caught in the feedback loop and unable to adapt, began to fall apart en masse. The battlefield was filled with the sounds of their destruction, a chaotic symphony of victory.

As the last of the Replicators disintegrated, the team breathed a collective sigh of relief. The weapon, enhanced by Asgard technology, had worked. The Replicator threat was finally over.

"We did it," Sarah Jane said, tears of relief in her eyes. "We actually did it."

Colonel O'Neill nodded, his face reflecting a mix of exhaustion and triumph. "Good job, everyone. We held the line."

Teal'c, ever stoic, added, "The Replicators are defeated. We have succeeded."

Jack Harkness grinned broadly. "That was one for the history books."

The Doctor, his hearts swelling with pride and gratitude, addressed his companions. "We faced impossible odds and emerged victorious. We did it together, as a team. The universe is safe because of all of you."

Thor's image reappeared, his expression reflecting the calm satisfaction of a job well done. "You have done well, Doctor. The Asgard are honored to have aided you in this fight. The Replicator threat is no more."

Kate Stewart, her face reflecting the weariness of battle but also immense pride, nodded. "UNIT, Torchwood, SG-1, and the Doctor's team—together, we achieved the impossible."

As the team regrouped and began to tend to the wounded and repair the damage, there was a sense of unity and triumph. They had faced a formidable enemy and won, standing together against the odds.

With the Replicator threat finally eliminated, the universe was safe once more. The Doctor and his companions knew that there would always be new challenges and adventures ahead, but they were ready to face them together.

As the TARDIS dematerialized, the Doctor looked at his friends, his eyes filled with hope. "Onward, to new adventures."

Rose, standing beside him, smiled. "To the end, Doctor."

With their spirits high and their resolve unwavering, the team looked forward to the future, ready to protect the universe from any threat, standing united until the very end.

Chapter 33: The Time Lord Offensive

The Citadel of the Time Lords on Gallifrey was a fortress of activity. The recent success against the Replicators had given the universe a fighting chance, but the battle was far from over. The Replicators, though severely weakened, still posed a significant threat, and the Time Lords had decided to take the offensive.

The Doctor, dressed in his Time Lord robes, stood before the High Council, his expression one of determination. Beside him were his companions: Rose, Jack Harkness, Sarah Jane, and SG-1. Rassilon, the Lord President, addressed the gathered Time Lords and their allies.

"Time Lords, our universe is under siege by a relentless enemy. The Replicators have adapted to every weapon we have thrown at them. But now, with the combined knowledge of Gallifrey and our allies, we shall launch a full-scale offensive and push them back for good."

The Doctor stepped forward, his voice filled with conviction. "We have the technology and the strategy to defeat them. The Asgard have given us the edge we need, and with the power of Gallifrey, we can strike at the heart of the Replicator threat."

Major Carter, holding a data pad with the latest schematics, added, "We've integrated the Asgard technology with Time Lord systems. This offensive will be a coordinated strike across multiple dimensions, targeting their core network."

Teal'c, his presence imposing and calm, said, "We must strike swiftly and decisively. The Replicators cannot be allowed to adapt."

The Doctor nodded. "And they won't. We'll use the TARDIS to deploy the enhanced Genesis Protocol across their network. The Time Lords will provide the temporal energy needed to power the assault."

Rassilon raised his staff, his voice echoing through the chamber. "Then let us prepare for battle. Time Lords, to your stations. We launch the offensive at once."

The Doctor and his team moved quickly, coordinating with the Time Lords and preparing the TARDIS for the assault. The TARDIS control room was a hive of activity as they integrated the latest upgrades and prepared for the massive temporal energy surge required for the offensive.

"Rose, Jack, I need you to monitor the power levels," the Doctor instructed. "We're going to be channeling a lot of energy."

"Got it, Doctor," Rose replied, taking her position by the console.

Jack Harkness nodded, his eyes gleaming with anticipation. "We're ready."

Major Carter and Daniel Jackson worked on finalizing the integration of the Asgard technology. "The key is to synchronize the temporal energy with the Genesis Protocol," Carter explained. "We'll create a temporal feedback loop that will disrupt their entire network."

The Doctor adjusted his sonic screwdriver, making the final calibrations. "We're almost there. Just a few more adjustments."

As the TARDIS powered up, the room filled with a low hum, the energy building to a crescendo. The viewscreen displayed the battlefield, where the Replicators were regrouping for another assault.

"All units, prepare for temporal insertion," the Doctor commanded. "We're about to take the fight to them."

The TARDIS dematerialized, reappearing in the heart of the Replicator stronghold. The combined forces of Gallifrey, UNIT, Torchwood, and SG-1 moved into position, ready to launch their assault.

Rassilon's voice echoed through the comms. "Time Lords, activate temporal disruptors. We shall create a temporal barrier to contain the Replicators."

The air shimmered as the Time Lords activated their devices, creating a shimmering temporal field that enveloped the battlefield. The Replicators, caught within the field, convulsed as their temporal cohesion was disrupted.

"Now, Doctor!" Rassilon commanded. "Deploy the Genesis Protocol."

The Doctor activated the enhanced Genesis Protocol, and a beam of pure, resonating energy shot out from the TARDIS, spreading through the temporal field. The Replicators convulsed, their forms breaking apart as the signal disrupted their core programming.

"It's working," Rose shouted, her voice filled with hope. "They're disintegrating!"

The Replicators, unable to adapt to the continuous temporal feedback loop, began to fall apart en masse. The combined firepower of the Time Lords and their allies created a devastating effect, pushing the Replicators back.

"Keep the pressure on!" Major Carter commanded. "We need to maintain the temporal barrier."

Teal'c, his staff weapon blazing, added, "We must not let them regroup."

The battlefield was a chaotic symphony of destruction as the Replicators were systematically dismantled. The temporal barrier prevented them from adapting, creating a perfect storm of devastation.

Jack Harkness, leading a squad of Torchwood operatives, grinned. "We've got them on the run!"

Sarah Jane, providing cover fire, added, "We need to push them back to their core."

The Doctor, his eyes focused on the viewscreen, saw the Replicators' central node. "There! That's their core network. If we take that out, we can end this."

Rassilon nodded. "Time Lords, focus all fire on the central node. We must destroy it."

The combined forces concentrated their firepower on the central node. The TARDIS, channeling the enhanced Genesis Protocol, created a beam of energy that pierced the heart of the Replicator network.

The Replicators convulsed violently, their forms disintegrating as the central node was destroyed. The feedback loop created a cascading failure, spreading through their entire network.

"It's over," the Doctor said, his voice filled with relief. "We've done it."

The battlefield fell silent as the last of the Replicators disintegrated. The temporal barrier shimmered and dissipated, the threat finally eliminated.

"We did it," Rose said, tears of relief in her eyes. "It's finally over."

Colonel O'Neill nodded, his face reflecting a mix of exhaustion and triumph. "Good job, everyone. We held the line."

Teal'c, ever stoic, added, "The Replicators are defeated. We have succeeded."

Jack Harkness grinned broadly. "That was one for the history books."

The Doctor, his hearts swelling with pride and gratitude, addressed his companions. "We faced impossible odds and emerged victorious. We did it together, as a team. The universe is safe because of all of you."

Rassilon's voice echoed through the comms, filled with respect. "You have done Gallifrey proud, Doctor. The Time Lords owe you and your allies a great debt."

Kate Stewart, her face reflecting the weariness of battle but also immense pride, nodded. "UNIT, Torchwood, SG-1, and the Doctor's team—together, we achieved the impossible."

As the team regrouped and began to tend to the wounded and repair the damage, there was a sense of unity and triumph. They had faced a formidable enemy and won, standing together against the odds.

With the Replicator threat finally eliminated, the universe was safe once more. The Doctor and his companions knew that there would always be new challenges and adventures ahead, but they were ready to face them together.

As the TARDIS dematerialized, the Doctor looked at his friends, his eyes filled with hope. "Onward, to new adventures."

Rose, standing beside him, smiled. "To the end, Doctor."

With their spirits high and their resolve unwavering, the team looked forward to the future, ready to protect the universe from any threat, standing united until the very end.

Chapter 34: The Heart of the Replicators

The TARDIS hummed with an almost ominous energy as it materialized in the central hub of Gallifrey. The recent victory had given them a momentary respite, but the Doctor knew the battle was far from over. The Replicators, while significantly weakened, still had a central hub—a heart—that drove their relentless quest for survival and adaptation. Destroying this hub would be the final blow to ensure their complete annihilation.

The Doctor gathered his closest allies: Rose, Jack Harkness, Sarah Jane, and the members of SG-1, around the central console. The Time Lords, represented by Rassilon, stood by, ready to provide whatever support was necessary.

"We've come a long way, and we've dealt a crippling blow to the Replicators," the Doctor began, his voice filled with urgency and determination. "But they have a central hub—a heart—that's still driving their adaptations. We need to find it and destroy it."

Rassilon, his face stern, nodded. "The Time Lords will provide you with all the resources you need, Doctor. Gallifrey stands ready to assist."

Major Carter, examining the data on her tablet, added, "We've been analyzing the Replicators' network. There's a concentration of signals that could be their central hub, located in a distant sector of space."

Daniel Jackson, cross-referencing the data, nodded in agreement. "It's heavily fortified, but if we can infiltrate it and plant the Genesis Protocol at the core, we can destroy them once and for all."

Teal'c, his expression stoic, said, "We must act swiftly. The Replicators will not wait for us to mount our offensive."

Colonel O'Neill, ever the pragmatist, added, "Alright, let's get to it. What's the plan, Doc?"

The Doctor adjusted his sonic screwdriver, his mind racing with possibilities. "We'll need to use the TARDIS to get us to the central hub. Once we're there, we'll deploy the Genesis Protocol directly into their core network. It's going to be dangerous, but it's our best chance."

Jack Harkness grinned, his confidence unwavering. "Dangerous is our specialty. Let's do this."

As the team prepared, the TARDIS powered up, the central console glowing with energy. The Doctor set the coordinates for the Replicators' central hub, and the TARDIS dematerialized, reappearing in the heart of the enemy stronghold.

The viewscreen displayed a vast, metallic structure, pulsating with a sinister energy. The Replicators' central hub was a labyrinthine network of conduits and nodes, each one teeming with activity.

"We're here," the Doctor announced. "Everyone, to your stations. This is it."

The team moved quickly, exiting the TARDIS and making their way through the maze-like corridors of the Replicator stronghold. The air was thick with the hum of machinery and the clatter of Replicator bodies moving in the shadows.

"Stay sharp," Colonel O'Neill warned, his weapon at the ready. "They know we're here."

As they advanced, they encountered heavy resistance. The Replicators, sensing the threat, attacked in swarms, their metallic forms glinting in the dim light.

"Engage!" O'Neill shouted, opening fire. "We need to keep moving!"

The team fought their way through the Replicators, their weapons blazing. Major Carter and Daniel Jackson worked together, using portable energy devices to disrupt the Replicators' network.

"We're close," Carter said, her voice tense. "The core should be just ahead."

The Doctor, using his sonic screwdriver, disabled the Replicators' defenses, creating a path to the central node. "This way! We need to plant the Genesis Protocol directly into their core."

As they reached the central chamber, they were met with a sight both awe-inspiring and terrifying. The core of the Replicator network was a massive, pulsating construct, its surface covered in writhing metallic tendrils.

"That's it," the Doctor said, his voice filled with determination. "The heart of the Replicators. We need to get the Genesis Protocol inside."

Teal'c, his staff weapon blazing, provided cover fire. "We must move quickly. The Replicators will not let us destroy their core without a fight."

Jack Harkness, leading the charge, shouted, "Sarah Jane, Rose, cover the Doctor and Carter! We need to hold them off!"

Rose and Sarah Jane fired their weapons, keeping the Replicators at bay while the Doctor and Carter approached the core. The Doctor adjusted the Genesis Protocol device, ready to deploy it.

"Just a little closer," the Doctor muttered, his hands steady despite the chaos around him.

Major Carter, working quickly, interfaced the device with the core. "We're ready. Deploying the Genesis Protocol... now!"

The device activated, sending a wave of energy through the Replicator core. The metallic tendrils convulsed, their structure destabilizing as the signal spread through the network.

"It's working!" Rose shouted, her voice filled with hope. "They're breaking apart!"

The Replicators convulsed violently, their forms disintegrating as the Genesis Protocol disrupted their core programming. The feedback loop created a cascading failure, spreading through the entire network.

"Keep the pressure on!" Major Carter commanded. "We need to maintain the signal until the core is completely destroyed."

The team continued to fight, holding off the Replicators as the Genesis Protocol did its work. The core began to fracture, cracks spreading across its surface as the energy wave intensified.

"We're almost there," the Doctor said, his eyes fixed on the core. "Just a little more."

The Replicators, unable to adapt to the continuous disruption, began to fall apart en masse. The core, now a mass of writhing metal, convulsed one last time before exploding in a burst of energy.

The shockwave knocked the team off their feet, but the Doctor, using his sonic screwdriver, quickly stabilized the energy field. The Replicators disintegrated, their network collapsing in on itself.

"It's over," the Doctor said, his voice filled with relief. "We've done it."

The battlefield fell silent as the last of the Replicators disintegrated. The team, battered but triumphant, regrouped and began to make their way back to the TARDIS.

"We did it," Sarah Jane said, tears of relief in her eyes. "It's finally over."

Colonel O'Neill nodded, his face reflecting a mix of exhaustion and triumph. "Good job, everyone. We held the line."

Teal'c, ever stoic, added, "The Replicators are defeated. We have succeeded."

Jack Harkness grinned broadly. "That was one for the history books."

The Doctor, his hearts swelling with pride and gratitude, addressed his companions. "We faced impossible odds and emerged victorious. We did it together, as a team. The universe is safe because of all of you."

Rassilon's voice echoed through the comms, filled with respect. "You have done Gallifrey proud, Doctor. The Time Lords owe you and your allies a great debt."

Kate Stewart, her face reflecting the weariness of battle but also immense pride, nodded. "UNIT, Torchwood, SG-1, and the Doctor's team—together, we achieved the impossible."

As the team regrouped and began to tend to the wounded and repair the damage, there was a sense of unity and triumph. They had faced a formidable enemy and won, standing together against the odds.

With the Replicator threat finally eliminated, the universe was safe once more. The Doctor and his companions knew that there would always be new challenges and adventures ahead, but they were ready to face them together.

As the TARDIS dematerialized, the Doctor looked at his friends, his eyes filled with hope. "Onward, to new adventures."

Rose, standing beside him, smiled. "To the end, Doctor."

With their spirits high and their resolve unwavering, the team looked forward to the future, ready to protect the universe from any threat, standing united until the very end.

Chapter 35: Infiltration

The TARDIS materialized on the outskirts of the Replicator hub, a massive, labyrinthine structure that seemed to pulse with a life of its own. The combined forces of SG-1, Torchwood, UNIT, and the Doctor stood ready, their faces set with determination. This was their final mission: to infiltrate the heart of the Replicator network and destroy it from within.

The Doctor, wearing his trademark long coat, gathered the team around the TARDIS console. "Alright, everyone. This is it. We're about to embark on the most dangerous mission yet. We need to infiltrate the Replicator hub, reach the core, and plant the Genesis Protocol directly into their central network."

Major Carter, her eyes focused and determined, added, "The Replicator hub is heavily fortified. We'll need to move quickly and quietly to avoid detection."

Colonel O'Neill, always the pragmatist, checked his weapon. "Alright, people, you heard the lady. Let's move out. Keep your eyes open and your heads down."

Teal'c, ever stoic, nodded. "We must remain vigilant. The Replicators will not be taken by surprise easily."

Jack Harkness, grinning confidently, adjusted his gear. "Let's show these tin cans what we're made of."

The team exited the TARDIS, moving swiftly and silently through the shadowy corridors of the Replicator hub. The walls were covered in a strange, shifting metallic substance, pulsating with a sinister energy. The air was filled with the faint hum of machinery and the distant clatter of Replicator bodies moving in the shadows.

"Stay close," the Doctor whispered, his sonic screwdriver in hand. "We need to reach the central node without triggering any alarms."

As they advanced, they encountered several patrols of Replicators. Major Carter and Daniel Jackson used portable energy devices to disable the Replicators' network connections, allowing the team to move past undetected.

"These energy pulses are disrupting their communications," Carter explained. "We should be able to move through without alerting the entire hub."

Daniel Jackson, scanning the area with a portable device, nodded. "The central node is just ahead. We need to disable the security measures before we can plant the Genesis Protocol."

The team moved carefully, disabling security measures and avoiding detection. They reached a large, heavily fortified chamber—the heart of the Replicator hub.

"This is it," the Doctor said, his voice low but filled with determination. "We need to plant the Genesis Protocol directly into the core."

Teal'c and Colonel O'Neill took point, their weapons ready. "We'll cover you," O'Neill said. "Get that protocol in place."

The Doctor, Major Carter, and Daniel Jackson moved to the core, a massive, pulsating construct that seemed to radiate malevolence. The Doctor used his sonic screwdriver to interface with the core, creating an opening to plant the device.

"Just a little more," the Doctor muttered, his hands steady despite the chaos around him.

Jack Harkness and Rose provided cover, firing at any Replicators that approached. "We've got your back, Doctor," Jack shouted. "Just get it done!"

Sarah Jane, her face set with determination, helped with the final connections. "We're almost there!"

Suddenly, an alarm blared through the hub, and Replicators swarmed into the chamber. The team was surrounded, but they fought valiantly, holding off the attackers.

"Keep them off us!" O'Neill shouted, firing his weapon. "We need more time!"

Teal'c, his staff weapon blazing, added, "We must not let them reach the Doctor."

The Doctor and Carter worked frantically to complete the installation. The core pulsed with energy, and the Replicators intensified their attack, sensing the threat.

"Doctor, we're running out of time!" Rose shouted, firing her weapon.

"Almost there!" the Doctor replied, his voice tense. "Just hold them off a little longer!"

With a final adjustment, the Doctor and Carter activated the Genesis Protocol. The device pulsed with energy, sending a wave of disruption through the core.

"It's done!" Carter shouted. "Get clear!"

The team retreated as the Genesis Protocol spread through the network, causing the Replicators to convulse and disintegrate. The core began to fracture, cracks spreading across its surface as the energy wave intensified.

"We need to get out of here!" the Doctor shouted. "Now!"

The team ran back through the corridors, dodging falling debris and disintegrating Replicator bodies. The TARDIS stood waiting, its doors open and welcoming.

"Everyone inside!" Jack shouted, covering the rear as the team piled into the TARDIS.

As the last of the team entered, the Doctor slammed the door shut and activated the controls. The TARDIS dematerialized just as the core exploded, sending a shockwave through the hub.

The TARDIS rematerialized safely back on Gallifrey, and the team stumbled out, exhausted but triumphant.

"We did it," Sarah Jane said, tears of relief in her eyes. "It's finally over."

Colonel O'Neill nodded, his face reflecting a mix of exhaustion and triumph. "Good job, everyone. We held the line."

Teal'c, ever stoic, added, "The Replicators are defeated. We have succeeded."

Jack Harkness grinned broadly. "That was one for the history books."

The Doctor, his hearts swelling with pride and gratitude, addressed his companions. "We faced impossible odds and emerged victorious. We did it together, as a team. The universe is safe because of all of you."

Rassilon's voice echoed through the comms, filled with respect. "You have done Gallifrey proud, Doctor. The Time Lords owe you and your allies a great debt."

Kate Stewart, her face reflecting the weariness of battle but also immense pride, nodded. "UNIT, Torchwood, SG-1, and the Doctor's team—together, we achieved the impossible."

As the team regrouped and began to tend to the wounded and repair the damage, there was a sense of unity and triumph. They had faced a formidable enemy and won, standing together against the odds.

With the Replicator threat finally eliminated, the universe was safe once more. The Doctor and his companions knew that there would always be new challenges and adventures ahead, but they were ready to face them together.

As the TARDIS dematerialized, the Doctor looked at his friends, his eyes filled with hope. "Onward, to new adventures."

Rose, standing beside him, smiled. "To the end, Doctor."

With their spirits high and their resolve unwavering, the team looked forward to the future, ready to protect the universe from any threat, standing united until the very end.

Chapter 36: The Final Battle Begins

The TARDIS stood at the heart of the UNIT command center, its blue exterior a beacon of hope amid the chaos. The Replicators, though weakened by the destruction of their central hub, had launched a desperate counteroffensive. The final battle was about to commence, and the combined forces of UNIT, Torchwood, SG-1, and the Doctor were preparing for the fight of their lives.

The Doctor, Rose, Jack Harkness, Sarah Jane, and the members of SG-1 gathered around a large holographic display, showing the latest intelligence on Replicator movements. Kate Stewart, her face set with determination, addressed the assembled teams.

"This is it, everyone. The Replicators are making their final stand. We need to hit them hard and fast. Our objective is to destroy their remaining strongholds and wipe them out for good."

The Doctor nodded, his eyes blazing with resolve. "We've come a long way and faced impossible odds, but we're still standing. This is our chance to end the threat once and for all."

Major Carter, her face focused and determined, added, "We'll need to coordinate our attacks and use the Genesis Protocol to disrupt their network. We've integrated the Asgard technology and the Time Lord temporal energy—this will be our most powerful assault yet."

Colonel O'Neill, ever the pragmatist, checked his weapon. "Alright, people, you heard the lady. Let's move out and show these Replicators what we're made of."

Teal'c, his presence imposing and calm, nodded. "We must strike swiftly and decisively. The Replicators cannot be allowed to regroup."

Jack Harkness, grinning confidently, adjusted his gear. "Let's give them hell."

The teams moved quickly, boarding their respective transports and preparing for the final assault. The TARDIS, acting as the central command and control, dematerialized and reappeared at the forefront of the battlefield.

The air was thick with tension as the combined forces deployed. The Replicators, sensing the impending attack, swarmed to defend their remaining strongholds. The ground shook with the force of the Replicator army, their metallic bodies glinting in the harsh light.

"All units, engage!" Kate Stewart commanded over the comms. "Remember your training and stick to the plan!"

Team One: UNIT and Torchwood

Colonel O'Neill, Major Carter, and Jack Harkness led the first wave, their weapons blazing. The UNIT and Torchwood soldiers moved with precision, targeting the Replicators' weak points.

"Focus fire on the central nodes!" O'Neill shouted. "We need to disrupt their communications!"

Major Carter, using a portable energy device, sent pulses through the Replicator ranks, causing them to convulse and break apart. "We're making progress! Keep pushing!"

Jack Harkness, ever the fearless leader, grinned as he fired his weapon. "Come on, you tin cans! Let's see what you've got!"

Sarah Jane, providing cover fire, added, "We need to get to their command center and plant the Genesis Protocol!"

Team Two: SG-1

Teal'c, Daniel Jackson, and Rose led the second wave, advancing through the chaotic battlefield. The Replicators, though formidable, were struggling to adapt to the relentless assault.

"Teal'c, take point!" Daniel shouted, firing his weapon. "We need to clear a path!"

Teal'c, his staff weapon blazing, moved with precision, taking down Replicators with each shot. "We must not let them regroup."

Rose, using a modified energy rifle, provided cover. "We're getting closer! The command center is just ahead!"

The Doctor's Command Team

The Doctor, coordinating the assault from the TARDIS, monitored the battle with intense focus. "Jack, Carter, I need you to deploy the Genesis Protocol now!"

"We're on it, Doctor!" Major Carter replied, her hands moving swiftly over the controls.

Jack Harkness, leading a squad of Torchwood operatives, reached the command center. "Planting the device now!"

The Genesis Protocol activated, sending a wave of disruptive energy through the Replicator network. The Replicators convulsed violently, their forms breaking apart as the signal spread.

"It's working!" Rose shouted, her voice filled with hope. "They're falling apart!"

But the Replicators, driven by desperation, launched a fierce counterattack. Swarms of metallic bodies surged towards the combined forces, their movements erratic and deadly.

"Hold the line!" Colonel O'Neill commanded. "We can't let them overwhelm us!"

Teal'c, his staff weapon blazing, added, "We must maintain our position. The Replicators are faltering."

Jack Harkness, firing relentlessly, grinned. "We've got them on the ropes! Just a little more!"

The battlefield was a chaotic symphony of destruction as the Replicators were systematically dismantled. The Genesis Protocol created a cascading failure, spreading through their entire network.

"Doctor, we're nearing the end," Major Carter reported. "The Replicators are breaking apart."

The Doctor, his eyes fixed on the viewscreen, saw the Replicators' command center. "There! That's the final node. We need to destroy it."

Rassilon's voice echoed through the comms. "Time Lords, focus all fire on the final node. This is our moment of victory."

The combined forces concentrated their firepower on the final node. The TARDIS, channeling the enhanced Genesis Protocol, created a beam of energy that pierced the heart of the Replicator network.

The Replicators convulsed violently, their forms disintegrating as the final node was destroyed. The feedback loop created a cascading failure, spreading through their entire network.

"It's over," the Doctor said, his voice filled with relief. "We've done it."

The battlefield fell silent as the last of the Replicators disintegrated. The team, battered but triumphant, regrouped and began to make their way back to the TARDIS.

"We did it," Sarah Jane said, tears of relief in her eyes. "It's finally over."

Colonel O'Neill nodded, his face reflecting a mix of exhaustion and triumph. "Good job, everyone. We held the line."

Teal'c, ever stoic, added, "The Replicators are defeated. We have succeeded."

Jack Harkness grinned broadly. "That was one for the history books."

The Doctor, his hearts swelling with pride and gratitude, addressed his companions. "We faced impossible odds and emerged victorious. We did it together, as a team. The universe is safe because of all of you."

Rassilon's voice echoed through the comms, filled with respect. "You have done Gallifrey proud, Doctor. The Time Lords owe you and your allies a great debt."

Kate Stewart, her face reflecting the weariness of battle but also immense pride, nodded. "UNIT, Torchwood, SG-1, and the Doctor's team—together, we achieved the impossible."

As the team regrouped and began to tend to the wounded and repair the damage, there was a sense of unity and triumph. They had faced a formidable enemy and won, standing together against the odds.

With the Replicator threat finally eliminated, the universe was safe once more. The Doctor and his companions knew that there would always be new challenges and adventures ahead, but they were ready to face them together.

As the TARDIS dematerialized, the Doctor looked at his friends, his eyes filled with hope. "Onward, to new adventures."

Rose, standing beside him, smiled. "To the end, Doctor."

With their spirits high and their resolve unwavering, the team looked forward to the future, ready to protect the universe from any threat, standing united until the very end.

Chapter 37: Sacrifices Made

The battlefield was eerily quiet after the final assault, but the remnants of the Replicators still posed a significant threat. The combined forces of UNIT, Torchwood, SG-1, and the Doctor regrouped to plan their next move. As they assessed the situation, it became clear that the fight was far from over.

The Doctor, Rose, Jack Harkness, Sarah Jane, and SG-1 gathered in the TARDIS, their faces grim but determined. Kate Stewart joined them via a secure video link from UNIT headquarters.

"The Replicators are weakened, but they're not defeated," the Doctor said, his voice filled with urgency. "We need to hit them with everything we've got. This is our last chance to end this once and for all."

Major Carter, her face set with determination, nodded. "We've identified several key nodes that are still active. If we can take them out, it will disrupt their network completely."

Teal'c, his expression stoic, added, "We must act swiftly. The Replicators will not give us another opportunity."

Colonel O'Neill, always the pragmatist, checked his weapon. "Alright, people, let's get to it. We know what we need to do."

The Doctor turned to Jack Harkness, his eyes filled with resolve. "Jack, I need you to lead the assault on the primary node. It's heavily fortified, but if we can take it out, it will cripple their defenses."

Jack grinned, his confidence unwavering. "You got it, Doctor. We'll give them hell."

Sarah Jane, standing beside the Doctor, added, "What about the secondary nodes? We need to hit them simultaneously."

Major Carter replied, "We'll split into two teams. SG-1 and UNIT will take one node, while Torchwood and the Doctor's team will take the other."

As they finalized their plans, the sense of urgency grew. They knew that sacrifices would have to be made to ensure victory.

The Assault Begins

The teams moved out, each heading to their designated targets. The TARDIS materialized near the primary node, its occupants ready for battle.

Jack Harkness led his Torchwood team through the chaotic corridors of the Replicator stronghold. The walls pulsed with a sinister energy, and the air was filled with the hum of machinery.

"Alright, everyone, stay sharp," Jack ordered. "We need to reach the core and plant the disruptor."

As they advanced, they encountered heavy resistance. Replicators swarmed towards them, their metallic forms glinting in the dim light.

"Engage!" Jack shouted, opening fire. "We need to keep moving!"

The team fought valiantly, but the Replicators' numbers were overwhelming. Jack realized that they wouldn't be able to reach the core without a significant distraction.

"Fall back!" he ordered, his voice filled with determination. "I'll hold them off. You get to the core and plant the disruptor."

"Jack, no!" Rose shouted, her eyes wide with fear. "You can't do this alone!"

Jack turned to her, his expression resolute. "It's the only way. Go, now!"

With a heavy heart, Rose and the team moved towards the core. Jack stayed behind, firing relentlessly at the approaching Replicators.

Team SG-1 and UNIT

Meanwhile, SG-1 and UNIT fought their way to the secondary node. Colonel O'Neill, Major Carter, Teal'c, and Daniel Jackson moved with precision, their weapons blazing.

"We're almost there," Carter shouted, her voice tense. "The node is just ahead!"

As they reached the node, they were met with fierce resistance. The Replicators swarmed towards them, their movements erratic and deadly.

"Keep them off us!" O'Neill ordered. "We need to plant the disruptor!"

Teal'c, his staff weapon blazing, provided cover fire. "We must not let them reach the node."

Daniel Jackson, using a portable energy device, worked quickly to interface with the node. "Just a little more..."

Suddenly, a Replicator swarm broke through their defenses, heading straight for the node. Major Carter realized they wouldn't be able to hold them off.

"Go!" she shouted. "I'll stay and buy you time!"

"Carter, no!" O'Neill shouted, his face filled with anguish. "We need you!"

Carter turned to him, her eyes filled with determination. "You need to finish this. Go!"

With a heavy heart, O'Neill and the team moved towards the node. Carter stayed behind, firing at the approaching Replicators with everything she had.

The Final Sacrifice

At the primary node, Rose and the team reached the core. They planted the disruptor, but the Replicators were closing in fast.

"We need to activate it now!" Rose shouted, her voice filled with urgency.

The Doctor, using his sonic screwdriver, activated the disruptor. A wave of energy spread through the node, causing the Replicators to convulse and disintegrate.

But the Replicators, driven by desperation, launched a final, ferocious assault. They swarmed towards the core, determined to stop the disruptor.

Jack, still fighting valiantly, realized what needed to be done. He activated a self-destruct device on his gear, creating a massive explosion that took out the remaining Replicators.

The shockwave knocked the team off their feet, but the node was destroyed. The Replicators' network began to collapse, their forms disintegrating as the signal spread.

"It's over," the Doctor said, his voice filled with relief. "We've done it."

As the battlefield fell silent, the team regrouped, their hearts heavy with the losses they had endured.

"We did it," Sarah Jane said, tears streaming down her face. "But at what cost?"

Colonel O'Neill, his face reflecting a mix of exhaustion and grief, nodded. "Good job, everyone. We held the line."

Teal'c, ever stoic, added, "Our comrades' sacrifices will not be in vain."

Rose, her eyes filled with sorrow, hugged the Doctor tightly. "Jack... he saved us all."

The Doctor, his hearts breaking for his friends, addressed the team. "We faced impossible odds and emerged victorious. We did it together, as a team. The universe is safe because of all of you."

Rassilon's voice echoed through the comms, filled with respect. "You have done Gallifrey proud, Doctor. The Time Lords owe you and your allies a great debt."

Kate Stewart, her face reflecting the weariness of battle but also immense pride, nodded. "UNIT, Torchwood, SG-1, and the Doctor's team—together, we achieved the impossible."

As the team tended to the wounded and began to repair the damage, there was a sense of unity and triumph, tempered by the loss of their comrades.

With the Replicator threat finally eliminated, the universe was safe once more. The Doctor and his companions knew that there would always be new challenges and adventures ahead, but they were ready to face them together, honoring the sacrifices made along the way.

As the TARDIS dematerialized, the Doctor looked at his friends, his eyes filled with hope. "Onward, to new adventures."

Rose, standing beside him, smiled through her tears. "To the end, Doctor."

With their spirits high and their resolve unwavering, the team looked forward to the future, ready to protect the universe from any threat, standing united until the very end, never forgetting the heroes who had given everything for their victory.

Chapter 38: Desperate Measures

The atmosphere inside the TARDIS was tense, filled with the hum of machinery and the low murmurs of the team as they planned their next move. The recent sacrifices of Jack Harkness and Major Carter weighed heavily on everyone's minds, but there was no time to grieve. The Replicators, though severely weakened, still clung to life, their central hub pulsating with malevolent energy.

The Doctor stood at the TARDIS console, his face grim and determined. He knew that they had to resort to desperate measures to end the threat once and for all. Rose, Sarah Jane, Teal'c, Daniel Jackson, and Colonel O'Neill were gathered around him, their expressions mirroring his resolve.

"We're running out of options," the Doctor said, his voice filled with urgency. "The Replicator hub is still active, and it's only a matter of time before they regroup and counterattack."

Colonel O'Neill, ever the pragmatist, nodded. "What's the plan, Doc? We need to hit them hard and fast."

The Doctor took a deep breath. "We need to destroy the hub from within. But to do that, we need to infiltrate it and plant a device powerful enough to create a cascading failure throughout their entire network."

Daniel Jackson, scanning the data on the viewscreen, added, "We've already disrupted their central nodes, but the core hub is still operational. If we can get to the core and deploy the Genesis Protocol one final time, it should collapse their entire structure."

Teal'c, his expression stoic, said, "The Replicators will not allow us to approach the core without resistance. We must be prepared for heavy combat."

Rose, her eyes filled with determination, looked at the Doctor. "We've come this far, Doctor. We can do this."

The Doctor nodded, his resolve unwavering. "There's one more thing. The Genesis Protocol alone might not be enough. We need to amplify it using the TARDIS's power source—the Eye of Harmony."

Sarah Jane gasped. "But Doctor, that could destroy the TARDIS!"

The Doctor's eyes were somber. "I know, but it's the only way. The Eye of Harmony has the power we need to amplify the Genesis Protocol and ensure the Replicator hub is completely destroyed."

Colonel O'Neill, his face set with determination, said, "Then let's do it. We're not losing anyone else today."

The Infiltration

The TARDIS materialized on the outskirts of the Replicator hub, its occupants ready for the final assault. The structure loomed ahead, a dark, pulsating mass of metal and energy.

"Alright, everyone," the Doctor said, his voice steady. "This is it. Stay close and watch each other's backs."

The team moved quickly, navigating the maze-like corridors of the Replicator hub. The walls were covered in shifting metallic tendrils, pulsating with a sinister energy. The air was filled with the hum of machinery and the distant clatter of Replicator bodies moving in the shadows.

As they advanced, they encountered heavy resistance. Swarms of Replicators surged towards them, their movements erratic and deadly.

"Engage!" O'Neill shouted, opening fire. "We need to keep moving!"

Teal'c, his staff weapon blazing, provided cover fire. "We must reach the core. The Replicators will not relent."

Daniel Jackson, using a portable energy device, sent pulses through the Replicator ranks, causing them to convulse and break apart. "We're getting closer!"

Rose and Sarah Jane fired their weapons, keeping the Replicators at bay. "Just a little more!" Rose shouted.

The Doctor, using his sonic screwdriver, disabled the Replicators' defenses, creating a path to the core. "This way! We need to plant the Genesis Protocol directly into their core network."

The Core

The team reached the central chamber, where the core of the Replicator network pulsed with a dark, ominous energy. The structure was massive, covered in writhing metallic tendrils.

"That's it," the Doctor said, his voice filled with determination. "The heart of the Replicators. We need to get the Genesis Protocol inside."

Colonel O'Neill and Teal'c took point, their weapons ready. "We'll cover you," O'Neill said. "Get that protocol in place."

The Doctor, Rose, and Daniel Jackson moved to the core, preparing to plant the device. The Replicators, sensing the threat, intensified their attack.

"Doctor, we're running out of time!" Rose shouted, firing her weapon.

The Doctor adjusted the Genesis Protocol device, his hands steady despite the chaos around him. "Almost there!"

Suddenly, a Replicator swarm broke through their defenses, heading straight for the core. The Doctor realized they wouldn't be able to hold them off.

"We need to amplify the signal now!" the Doctor shouted. "Rose, help me with the Eye of Harmony."

Rose nodded, her face set with determination. "Let's do this."

The Doctor and Rose accessed the TARDIS's power source, the Eye of Harmony. The core pulsed with energy, and the Replicators intensified their attack, sensing the imminent threat.

"Just a little more," the Doctor muttered, his hands moving swiftly over the controls. "We need to synchronize the Genesis Protocol with the Eye of Harmony."

The energy from the Eye of Harmony began to flow into the Genesis Protocol, amplifying its power. The device pulsed with a blinding light, sending a wave of disruption through the Replicator core.

"It's working!" Daniel shouted, his voice filled with hope. "The Replicators are breaking apart!"

But the Replicators, driven by desperation, launched a final, ferocious assault. Swarms of metallic bodies surged towards the team, determined to stop the disruptor.

"Hold the line!" O'Neill commanded. "We can't let them overwhelm us!"

Teal'c, his staff weapon blazing, added, "We must maintain our position. The Replicators are faltering."

Rose, her eyes filled with determination, stayed by the Doctor's side, helping to stabilize the energy flow. "We're almost there, Doctor!"

The core began to fracture, cracks spreading across its surface as the energy wave intensified. The Replicators convulsed violently, their forms disintegrating as the Genesis Protocol and the Eye of Harmony's energy spread through the network.

The Sacrifice

The Doctor realized that the energy from the Eye of Harmony was destabilizing the TARDIS. "Rose, we need to disconnect the Eye of Harmony, or we'll lose the TARDIS!"

Rose nodded, tears streaming down her face. "But if we do, the Genesis Protocol might not be powerful enough!"

The Doctor's eyes were filled with sorrow and determination. "We have to try. We can't lose the TARDIS."

As they worked to disconnect the Eye of Harmony, the TARDIS began to shake violently. The energy from the core was too much for the ship to handle.

"We need more time!" the Doctor shouted. "Just a few more seconds!"

Colonel O'Neill, seeing the danger, made a split-second decision. "Doctor, get everyone out of here. We'll hold them off."

"No!" the Doctor shouted. "I won't leave you behind!"

O'Neill's face was set with determination. "You have to. It's the only way. Go!"

With a heavy heart, the Doctor and Rose disconnected the Eye of Harmony, stabilizing the TARDIS. The Genesis Protocol continued to spread through the Replicator network, but the TARDIS began to dematerialize, taking the team with it.

As the TARDIS rematerialized on Gallifrey, the Doctor collapsed to his knees, his hearts breaking for his friends left behind. The Replicator core, now fully destabilized, exploded, sending a shockwave through the hub.

The Replicators convulsed violently, their forms disintegrating as the feedback loop created a cascading failure. The threat was finally over.

The Aftermath

The team regrouped, their hearts heavy with the sacrifices made. The Replicator threat had been eliminated, but the cost had been high.

"We did it," Sarah Jane said, tears streaming down her face. "But at what cost?"

Colonel O'Neill, battered but alive, stepped forward. "We held the line. We did what we had to do."

Teal'c, ever stoic, nodded. "Our comrades' sacrifices will not be in vain."

Rose, her eyes filled with sorrow, hugged the Doctor tightly. "We lost so many."

The Doctor, his hearts breaking for his friends, addressed the team. "We faced impossible odds and emerged victorious. We did it together, as a team. The universe is safe because of all of you."

Rassilon's voice echoed through the comms, filled with respect. "You have done Gallifrey proud, Doctor. The Time Lords owe you and your allies a great debt."

Kate Stewart, her face reflecting the weariness of battle but also immense pride, nodded. "UNIT, Torchwood, SG-1, and the Doctor's team—together, we achieved the impossible."

As the team tended to the wounded and began to repair the damage, there was a sense of unity and triumph, tempered by the loss of their comrades.

With the Replicator threat finally eliminated, the universe was safe once more. The Doctor and his companions knew that there would always be new challenges and adventures ahead, but they were ready to face them together, honoring the sacrifices made along the way.

As the TARDIS dematerialized, the Doctor looked at his friends, his eyes filled with hope. "Onward, to new adventures."

Rose, standing beside him, smiled through her tears. "To the end, Doctor."

With their spirits high and their resolve unwavering, the team looked forward to the future, ready to protect the universe from any threat, standing united until the very end, never forgetting the heroes who had given everything for their victory.

Chapter 39: A New Threat

The sense of victory that filled the air was palpable. The combined forces of UNIT, Torchwood, SG-1, and the Doctor had fought valiantly and finally destroyed the Replicator hub, ending their immediate threat. However, the respite was brief. The TARDIS, once a sanctuary, now hummed with an ominous energy, signaling that something was terribly wrong.

The Doctor, Rose, Jack Harkness, Sarah Jane, and SG-1 gathered in the TARDIS control room, their faces lined with exhaustion but also relief. The Doctor was at the console, scanning the surrounding space-time for any remaining Replicator activity.

"Doctor, what's going on?" Rose asked, noticing the Doctor's increasingly worried expression.

The Doctor's face was grave. "I'm picking up a strange signal. It's unlike anything I've seen before. It's a new form of Replicators—more advanced and far more dangerous."

Colonel O'Neill, standing with his arms crossed, frowned. "More dangerous? How can they be more dangerous than the ones we just destroyed?"

Major Carter, scanning the data on the viewscreen, added, "The signal indicates that these new Replicators have adapted to our previous tactics. They've evolved again, and this time, they're not just mechanical —they've integrated organic components."

Daniel Jackson, his face pale with realization, said, "Organic components? That means they can heal and adapt even faster than before."

Teal'c, ever stoic, nodded. "We must prepare for their assault. They will not give us time to regroup."

Jack Harkness, his usual bravado tinged with concern, grinned. "Alright, team. Looks like we've got a new challenge. Let's show these Replicators what we're made of."

The Doctor's fingers flew over the controls, his mind racing. "We need to develop a new strategy. The old methods won't work on these new Replicators. We'll need to use everything we've got."

Kate Stewart's voice came through the comms, filled with urgency. "Doctor, we're detecting large-scale Replicator movements across multiple sectors. They're converging on our position."

The Doctor nodded, his face set with determination. "Alright, everyone. This is it. We're facing an enemy unlike any we've seen before. But we've got the best team in the universe. Let's get to work."

The First Assault

The TARDIS materialized in the heart of the battlefield, its occupants ready for the fight of their lives. The air was thick with tension as the combined forces deployed, their weapons primed and ready.

As they stepped out, they were met with a terrifying sight. The new Replicators were larger, more menacing, with a horrifying combination of metallic and organic components. Their bodies pulsated with a sinister energy, and their eyes glowed with malevolence.

"Engage!" O'Neill shouted, opening fire. "Don't let them get close!"

The combined forces fired their weapons, but the new Replicators seemed almost impervious to the energy blasts. They moved with terrifying speed, their organic components healing almost instantly.

"We need to find a new strategy," Carter shouted, her voice filled with urgency. "Our weapons aren't having any effect!"

The Doctor, using his sonic screwdriver, scanned the new Replicators. "Their organic components are acting as a regenerative matrix. We need to disrupt their internal network. Rose, Jack, Sarah Jane, follow me!"

The team fought their way through the chaos, the new Replicators closing in from all sides. The Doctor led them to a makeshift command post, where they began working on a new plan.

"We need to create a disruption field," the Doctor explained, his hands moving swiftly over the controls. "Something that can interfere with their regenerative matrix."

Sarah Jane, examining the data, added, "We can use the TARDIS's temporal energy to create a field that will disrupt their healing process."

Jack Harkness grinned. "Sounds like a plan. Let's get to it."

The Counterattack

The team worked quickly, integrating the new technology with the TARDIS's systems. The Doctor calibrated the temporal energy field, preparing to deploy it against the new Replicators.

"Everyone, get ready!" the Doctor shouted. "We're about to activate the field."

As the field activated, a wave of energy spread across the battlefield. The new Replicators convulsed, their regenerative matrix disrupted. For the first time, they showed signs of vulnerability.

"It's working!" Rose shouted, her voice filled with hope. "They're breaking apart!"

But the new Replicators, driven by desperation, launched a ferocious counterattack. Swarms of metallic and organic bodies surged towards the combined forces, their movements erratic and deadly.

"Hold the line!" O'Neill commanded. "We can't let them overwhelm us!"

Teal'c, his staff weapon blazing, added, "We must maintain our position. The Replicators are faltering."

Jack Harkness, firing relentlessly, grinned. "We've got them on the ropes! Just a little more!"

The Final Push

The battlefield was a chaotic symphony of destruction as the new Replicators were systematically dismantled. The temporal disruption field created a cascading failure, spreading through their entire network.

The Doctor, his eyes fixed on the viewscreen, saw the new Replicators' command center. "There! That's the final node. We need to destroy it."

Rassilon's voice echoed through the comms. "Time Lords, focus all fire on the final node. This is our moment of victory."

The combined forces concentrated their firepower on the final node. The TARDIS, channeling the enhanced temporal energy, created a beam of energy that pierced the heart of the Replicator network.

The new Replicators convulsed violently, their forms disintegrating as the final node was destroyed. The feedback loop created a cascading failure, spreading through their entire network.

"It's over," the Doctor said, his voice filled with relief. "We've done it."

The battlefield fell silent as the last of the new Replicators disintegrated. The team, battered but triumphant, regrouped and began to make their way back to the TARDIS.

"We did it," Sarah Jane said, tears streaming down her face. "It's finally over."

Colonel O'Neill nodded, his face reflecting a mix of exhaustion and triumph. "Good job, everyone. We held the line."

Teal'c, ever stoic, added, "The Replicators are defeated. We have succeeded."

Jack Harkness grinned broadly. "That was one for the history books."

The Doctor, his hearts swelling with pride and gratitude, addressed his companions. "We faced impossible odds and emerged victorious. We did it together, as a team. The universe is safe because of all of you."

Rassilon's voice echoed through the comms, filled with respect. "You have done Gallifrey proud, Doctor. The Time Lords owe you and your allies a great debt."

Kate Stewart, her face reflecting the weariness of battle but also immense pride, nodded. "UNIT, Torchwood, SG-1, and the Doctor's team—together, we achieved the impossible."

As the team tended to the wounded and began to repair the damage, there was a sense of unity and triumph. They had faced a formidable enemy and won, standing together against the odds.

With the Replicator threat finally eliminated, the universe was safe once more. The Doctor and his companions knew that there would always be new challenges and adventures ahead, but they were ready to face them together.

As the TARDIS dematerialized, the Doctor looked at his friends, his eyes filled with hope. "Onward, to new adventures."

Rose, standing beside him, smiled. "To the end, Doctor."

With their spirits high and their resolve unwavering, the team looked forward to the future, ready to protect the universe from any threat, standing united until the very end.

Chapter 40: Ancient Wisdom

The TARDIS hummed with an eerie sense of anticipation as it traveled through the vortex. The team had managed to defeat the new wave of Replicators, but the battle had taken its toll. The Replicators had evolved again, becoming even more formidable. The Doctor knew they needed a new strategy, one rooted in ancient wisdom.

The Doctor gathered his closest allies—Rose, Jack Harkness, Sarah Jane, and SG-1—in the TARDIS control room. The holographic display showed the remnants of the Replicator threat still looming large.

"Doctor, what's our next move?" Rose asked, her eyes filled with concern.

The Doctor's face was etched with determination. "We need to consult the ancient beings—the ones who seeded life in the universe. They possess knowledge far beyond our understanding. If anyone can help us defeat these new Replicators, it's them."

Daniel Jackson, his expertise in ancient languages and cultures invaluable, stepped forward. "Doctor, I think I know where we can find the information we need. The Ancients, or the Alterans as they were originally known, left behind vast repositories of knowledge. One of these repositories is located on an ancient planet known as Dakara."

Colonel O'Neill, ever the pragmatist, nodded. "Alright, let's get to it. Time's not on our side."

Teal'c, his expression stoic, added, "The Replicators will not wait for us to find a solution. We must act swiftly."

Jack Harkness grinned, his confidence unshaken. "Let's show these ancient beings what we're made of."

The Doctor set the coordinates, and the TARDIS dematerialized, reappearing in the ruins of Dakara. The planet was ancient, its surface covered in the remnants of a once-great civilization.

"Alright, everyone," the Doctor said, his voice steady. "Stay close. We need to find the repository and access its knowledge."

The Search for Wisdom

The team moved carefully through the ruins, their weapons at the ready. The air was filled with the hum of ancient machinery and the distant echoes of a forgotten past.

"This place is incredible," Daniel said, his eyes wide with wonder. "The Ancients left so much behind."

As they explored the ruins, they encountered various traps and defenses left by the Ancients to protect their knowledge. Teal'c and O'Neill disabled the traps with precision, allowing the team to move forward.

"We're close," Daniel said, consulting his notes. "The repository should be just ahead."

They reached a large chamber, its walls covered in intricate carvings and glowing symbols. In the center of the chamber stood a pedestal with a glowing crystal.

"That's it," Daniel said, his voice filled with excitement. "The repository of the Ancients."

The Doctor approached the pedestal, using his sonic screwdriver to interface with the crystal. The chamber filled with light as the repository activated, revealing a vast library of knowledge.

The Consultation

As the team began to search through the repository, Daniel and the Doctor focused on the ancient texts, translating the information.

"Doctor, look at this," Daniel said, pointing to a series of symbols. "The Ancients developed an energy weapon with frequency fluctuation. It was designed to seed life in the universe, but it can also disrupt and destroy artificial lifeforms."

The Doctor's eyes lit up with realization. "That's it! We can use this weapon against the Replicators. The frequency fluctuation will prevent them from adapting."

Rose, her face filled with hope, asked, "Can we build it?"

The Doctor nodded, his mind racing with possibilities. "We have the technology. We just need to integrate the TARDIS's systems with the ancient weapon."

Jack Harkness grinned. "Sounds like a plan. Let's get to work."

The Construction

The team returned to the TARDIS, where they began the intricate process of constructing the ancient energy weapon. The Doctor and Daniel worked side by side, translating the ancient texts and integrating the TARDIS's technology.

"We need to ensure the frequency fluctuation is precise," Daniel explained. "Even a small error could render the weapon ineffective."

The Doctor adjusted the controls with his sonic screwdriver. "The TARDIS's temporal matrix should help stabilize the frequency. We'll use the Eye of Harmony to power the weapon."

As they worked, the atmosphere was charged with anticipation. The team knew that this weapon was their last hope to defeat the new Replicators.

The Final Battle

With the weapon complete, the TARDIS materialized on the battle-field where the Replicators were amassing for a final assault. The air was thick with tension as the combined forces of UNIT, Torchwood, and SG-1 prepared for the fight.

"Everyone, to your positions," the Doctor commanded. "This is our last chance."

The team deployed the ancient energy weapon, its glowing core pulsating with energy. The Replicators surged forward, their new forms more terrifying than ever.

"Engage!" O'Neill shouted, opening fire. "We need to hold them off until the weapon is ready!"

Teal'c, his staff weapon blazing, provided cover fire. "We must protect the weapon at all costs."

Jack Harkness, firing relentlessly, grinned. "Let's give them hell!"

Rose and Sarah Jane, working alongside the Doctor, monitored the weapon's power levels. "We're at 75% capacity," Rose reported. "Almost there!"

The Doctor, his eyes fixed on the viewscreen, adjusted the controls. "Just a little more. We need to synchronize the frequency fluctuation."

As the weapon reached full power, the Doctor activated it. A beam of pure, resonating energy shot out, enveloping the Replicator swarm. The frequency fluctuation disrupted their forms, preventing them from adapting.

"It's working!" Rose shouted, her voice filled with hope. "They're breaking apart!"

The Replicators convulsed violently, their forms disintegrating as the energy wave spread through their ranks. The battlefield was filled with the sounds of their destruction, a chaotic symphony of victory.

"Keep the pressure on!" O'Neill commanded. "We're almost there!"

Teal'c, ever calm, added, "We must not relent."

As the last of the Replicators disintegrated, the team breathed a collective sigh of relief. The weapon had worked, and the threat was finally over.

The Aftermath

The team regrouped, their faces filled with exhaustion but also triumph. The Replicator threat had been eliminated, thanks to the ancient wisdom and their unwavering determination.

"We did it," Sarah Jane said, tears streaming down her face. "It's finally over."

Colonel O'Neill nodded, his face reflecting a mix of exhaustion and triumph. "Good job, everyone. We held the line."

Teal'c, ever stoic, added, "The Replicators are defeated. We have succeeded."

Jack Harkness grinned broadly. "That was one for the history books."

The Doctor, his hearts swelling with pride and gratitude, addressed his companions. "We faced impossible odds and emerged victorious. We did it together, as a team. The universe is safe because of all of you."

Rassilon's voice echoed through the comms, filled with respect. "You have done Gallifrey proud, Doctor. The Time Lords owe you and your allies a great debt."

Kate Stewart, her face reflecting the weariness of battle but also immense pride, nodded. "UNIT, Torchwood, SG-1, and the Doctor's team—together, we achieved the impossible."

As the team tended to the wounded and began to repair the damage, there was a sense of unity and triumph. They had faced a formidable enemy and won, standing together against the odds.

With the Replicator threat finally eliminated, the universe was safe once more. The Doctor and his companions knew that there would always be new challenges and adventures ahead, but they were ready to face them together, honoring the sacrifices made along the way.

As the TARDIS dematerialized, the Doctor looked at his friends, his eyes filled with hope. "Onward, to new adventures."

Rose, standing beside him, smiled through her tears. "To the end, Doctor."

With their spirits high and their resolve unwavering, the team looked forward to the future, ready to protect the universe from any threat, standing united until the very end, never forgetting the heroes who had given everything for their victory.

Chapter 41: The Ultimate Plan

The TARDIS hummed with a sense of urgent purpose as the combined forces of UNIT, Torchwood, and SG-1 gathered once more in the control room. The recent victory over the new Replicators had given them hope, but the threat was far from eliminated. The Replicators had scattered, retreating to hidden strongholds across the universe. The Doctor knew they needed an ultimate plan to eradicate the Replicators once and for all.

The Doctor, Rose, Jack Harkness, Sarah Jane, and SG-1 stood around the central console, their faces lined with determination. Kate Stewart's image flickered on the holographic display, coordinating from UNIT headquarters.

"We need a plan to end this once and for all," the Doctor began, his voice steady but intense. "The Replicators are scattered, but they'll regroup if we give them time. We need to strike simultaneously across the universe."

Daniel Jackson, his expertise in ancient technologies crucial, stepped forward. "Doctor, the Ancients left behind technology that could help us. Combined with Time Lord and Asgard technology, we can create a weapon powerful enough to wipe out the Replicators completely."

Major Carter, always thinking ahead, nodded. "We can integrate the temporal energy of the TARDIS with the Asgard's energy modulation and the Ancients' weaponry. This combination will be our ultimate weapon."

Colonel O'Neill, ever the pragmatist, added, "Alright, let's get to it. Time's not on our side."

Teal'c, his expression stoic, said, "The Replicators will not wait for us to devise a plan. We must act swiftly."

Jack Harkness, grinning confidently, adjusted his gear. "Let's show these Replicators what we're made of."

The Doctor activated the TARDIS's temporal scanners, searching for the scattered Replicator strongholds. "We need to synchronize our attack to ensure they don't have time to adapt. We'll deploy the ultimate weapon simultaneously across the universe."

The Assembly

The team split into groups, each tasked with a critical part of the plan. Major Carter and Daniel Jackson focused on integrating the Ancients' technology with the TARDIS's systems, while Teal'c and O'Neill prepared the ground forces for the final assault.

"We need to ensure the frequency modulation is precise," Carter explained, adjusting the controls. "The TARDIS's temporal energy will help stabilize the weapon."

Daniel Jackson, translating the ancient texts, added, "The Ancients' weaponry is designed to disrupt and destroy artificial lifeforms. Combined with the Asgard's energy modulation, it will be unstoppable."

The Doctor, using his sonic screwdriver, calibrated the systems. "We'll channel the energy through the TARDIS's temporal matrix. It will amplify the weapon's power and spread the signal across the universe."

Rose and Jack worked on coordinating the logistics, ensuring that every team was in position. "We need to hit them hard and fast," Rose said, her eyes filled with determination. "This is our last chance."

The Deployment

With the ultimate weapon ready, the TARDIS materialized in the heart of the battlefield. The combined forces of UNIT, Torchwood, and SG-1 stood ready, their weapons primed and their resolve unwavering.

"Alright, everyone," the Doctor said, his voice carrying a sense of finality. "This is it. We're going to end this once and for all. Stay sharp and watch each other's backs."

The TARDIS began to hum with a powerful energy as the temporal matrix synchronized with the Ancients' weaponry and the Asgard's energy modulation. The ultimate weapon was ready to deploy.

"All units, prepare for simultaneous deployment," Kate Stewart commanded over the comms. "We need to strike all the strongholds at once."

As the TARDIS powered up, the Doctor activated the weapon. A beam of pure, resonating energy shot out, enveloping the Replicator strongholds. The frequency modulation and temporal energy created a cascading disruption, preventing the Replicators from adapting.

"It's working!" Rose shouted, her voice filled with hope. "They're breaking apart!"

The Replicators convulsed violently, their forms disintegrating as the energy wave spread through their ranks. The battlefield was filled with the sounds of their destruction, a chaotic symphony of victory.

"Keep the pressure on!" O'Neill commanded. "We're almost there!"

Teal'c, ever calm, added, "We must not relent."

The ultimate weapon created a feedback loop, spreading through the Replicators' network and causing a catastrophic failure. The strongholds began to collapse, their forms disintegrating into dust.

The Final Push

The combined forces advanced, taking advantage of the Replicators' weakened state. The TARDIS, channeling the ultimate weapon's power, continued to spread the signal, ensuring that no Replicator stronghold was left untouched.

"We're nearing the end," Carter reported, monitoring the readings. "The Replicators' network is collapsing."

The Doctor, his eyes fixed on the viewscreen, saw the final stronghold. "There! That's the last one. We need to destroy it completely."

Rassilon's voice echoed through the comms. "Time Lords, focus all fire on the final stronghold. This is our moment of victory."

The combined forces concentrated their firepower on the final stronghold. The TARDIS, channeling the enhanced temporal energy, created a beam of energy that pierced the heart of the Replicator network.

The Replicators convulsed violently, their forms disintegrating as the final node was destroyed. The feedback loop created a cascading failure, spreading through their entire network.

"It's over," the Doctor said, his voice filled with relief. "We've done it."

The battlefield fell silent as the last of the Replicators disintegrated. The team, battered but triumphant, regrouped and began to make their way back to the TARDIS.

"We did it," Sarah Jane said, tears streaming down her face. "It's finally over."

Colonel O'Neill nodded, his face reflecting a mix of exhaustion and triumph. "Good job, everyone. We held the line."

Teal'c, ever stoic, added, "The Replicators are defeated. We have succeeded."

Jack Harkness grinned broadly. "That was one for the history books."

The Aftermath

The team regrouped, their faces filled with exhaustion but also triumph. The Replicator threat had been eliminated, thanks to the combination of Time Lord, Asgard, and Ancient technology, and their unwavering determination.

The Doctor, his hearts swelling with pride and gratitude, addressed his companions. "We faced impossible odds and emerged victorious. We did it together, as a team. The universe is safe because of all of you."

Rassilon's voice echoed through the comms, filled with respect. "You have done Gallifrey proud, Doctor. The Time Lords owe you and your allies a great debt."

Kate Stewart, her face reflecting the weariness of battle but also immense pride, nodded. "UNIT, Torchwood, SG-1, and the Doctor's team—together, we achieved the impossible."

As the team tended to the wounded and began to repair the damage, there was a sense of unity and triumph. They had faced a formidable enemy and won, standing together against the odds.

With the Replicator threat finally eliminated, the universe was safe once more. The Doctor and his companions knew that there would always be new challenges and adventures ahead, but they were ready to face them together.

As the TARDIS dematerialized, the Doctor looked at his friends, his eyes filled with hope. "Onward, to new adventures."

Rose, standing beside him, smiled. "To the end, Doctor."

With their spirits high and their resolve unwavering, the team looked forward to the future, ready to protect the universe from any threat, standing united until the very end, never forgetting the heroes who had given everything for their victory.

Chapter 42: Execution of the Plan

The TARDIS materialized with a reassuring thud in the command center of UNIT headquarters. The air was electric with anticipation. The combined forces of UNIT, Torchwood, and SG-1 were ready to execute their ultimate plan to eradicate the Replicators once and for all.

The Doctor stood at the central console, his face a mask of determination. Around him were Rose, Jack Harkness, Sarah Jane, and SG-1, each prepared for the roles they would play in this final battle. Kate Stewart coordinated from the command center, her voice crisp and clear over the comms.

"Alright, everyone," the Doctor began, his voice steady and resolute. "This is it. We've devised the ultimate plan, and now it's time to put it into action. We need to strike all the Replicator strongholds simultaneously. Our success depends on perfect synchronization and flawless execution."

Colonel O'Neill, ever the pragmatic leader, checked his weapon and gave a curt nod. "You heard the man. Let's get to it."

Major Carter, her eyes gleaming with determination, added, "Remember, our goal is to disrupt and destroy their network completely. No margin for error."

Teal'c, his expression stoic, said, "The Replicators will not give us another chance. We must act swiftly and decisively."

Jack Harkness, grinning with his usual bravado, adjusted his gear. "Let's give these Replicators a run for their money."

Daniel Jackson, holding a portable device containing the translated ancient texts, spoke up. "Doctor, the frequency modulation is set. We're ready to deploy the weapon."

The Doctor nodded, his eyes fixed on the holographic display showing the locations of the Replicator strongholds. "Alright, everyone. Take your positions. We move on my mark."

The Deployment

The TARDIS dematerialized and reappeared at the first Replicator stronghold. The combined forces moved swiftly, each team executing their roles with precision. The air was filled with the hum of advanced technology and the low murmur of tactical communications.

"Team Alpha, in position," O'Neill reported over the comms.

"Team Bravo, ready to move," Carter added.

"Team Charlie, standing by," Teal'c confirmed.

The Doctor, standing at the heart of the TARDIS, monitored the synchronization of the teams. "Activate the temporal synchronization field. We need to ensure that all teams strike simultaneously."

Rose, standing beside him, worked quickly to adjust the controls. "Synchronization field activated, Doctor."

The TARDIS hummed with a powerful energy as the temporal synchronization field spread across the battlefield, ensuring that all teams would strike at the exact same moment.

"On my mark," the Doctor commanded. "Three, two, one—mark!"

The Assault

The combined forces surged forward, their weapons blazing. The Replicators, caught off guard by the sudden, synchronized assault, convulsed as the energy waves disrupted their network.

"Engage!" O'Neill shouted, leading the charge. "Take out those nodes!"

Major Carter, using her portable energy device, targeted the Replicators' communication nodes. "Disrupt their network! They can't adapt if we keep the pressure on!"

Teal'c, his staff weapon blazing, moved with precision, taking down Replicators with each shot. "We must not let them regroup."

Jack Harkness, grinning confidently, led his team through the chaotic battlefield. "Keep moving! We need to reach the core!"

Sarah Jane, providing cover fire, added, "We're almost there! Stay focused!"

The Core

As the teams advanced, they converged on the central core of the Replicator network. The structure was massive, pulsating with a sinister energy. The air was thick with the hum of machinery and the clatter of Replicator bodies.

"That's it," the Doctor said, his voice filled with determination. "The heart of the Replicators. We need to plant the device and activate the weapon."

Daniel Jackson, translating the final instructions, nodded. "We need to interface the device with the core and ensure the frequency modulation is precise."

The Doctor, using his sonic screwdriver, adjusted the device. "Rose, Jack, keep them off us. We need a few more minutes."

Rose and Jack fired their weapons, holding back the waves of Replicators that surged towards them. "We've got your back, Doctor," Rose shouted.

Sarah Jane, working alongside the Doctor, helped to stabilize the device. "Almost there!"

The Doctor and Daniel Jackson worked frantically to integrate the device with the core. The energy from the TARDIS's temporal matrix and the Asgard's energy modulation flowed into the device, amplifying its power.

"Just a little more," the Doctor muttered, his hands moving swiftly over the controls. "We need to synchronize the frequency fluctuation."

The Activation

With a final adjustment, the Doctor activated the device. A beam of pure, resonating energy shot out, enveloping the Replicator core. The frequency modulation disrupted their forms, preventing them from adapting.

"It's working!" Rose shouted, her voice filled with hope. "They're breaking apart!"

The Replicators convulsed violently, their forms disintegrating as the energy wave spread through their ranks. The battlefield was filled with the sounds of their destruction, a chaotic symphony of victory.

"Keep the pressure on!" O'Neill commanded. "We're almost there!"

Teal'c, ever calm, added, "We must not relent."

The ultimate weapon created a feedback loop, spreading through the Replicators' network and causing a catastrophic failure. The strongholds began to collapse, their forms disintegrating into dust.

"We're nearing the end," Carter reported, monitoring the readings. "The Replicators' network is collapsing."

The Doctor, his eyes fixed on the viewscreen, saw the final stronghold. "There! That's the last one. We need to destroy it completely."

Rassilon's voice echoed through the comms. "Time Lords, focus all fire on the final stronghold. This is our moment of victory."

The combined forces concentrated their firepower on the final stronghold. The TARDIS, channeling the enhanced temporal energy, created a beam of energy that pierced the heart of the Replicator network.

The Replicators convulsed violently, their forms disintegrating as the final node was destroyed. The feedback loop created a cascading failure, spreading through their entire network.

"It's over," the Doctor said, his voice filled with relief. "We've done it."

The Aftermath

The battlefield fell silent as the last of the Replicators disintegrated. The team, battered but triumphant, regrouped and began to make their way back to the TARDIS.

"We did it," Sarah Jane said, tears streaming down her face. "It's finally over."

Colonel O'Neill nodded, his face reflecting a mix of exhaustion and triumph. "Good job, everyone. We held the line."

Teal'c, ever stoic, added, "The Replicators are defeated. We have succeeded."

Jack Harkness grinned broadly. "That was one for the history books."

The Doctor, his hearts swelling with pride and gratitude, addressed his companions. "We faced impossible odds and emerged victorious. We did it together, as a team. The universe is safe because of all of you."

Rassilon's voice echoed through the comms, filled with respect. "You have done Gallifrey proud, Doctor. The Time Lords owe you and your allies a great debt."

Kate Stewart, her face reflecting the weariness of battle but also immense pride, nodded. "UNIT, Torchwood, SG-1, and the Doctor's team—together, we achieved the impossible."

As the team tended to the wounded and began to repair the damage, there was a sense of unity and triumph. They had faced a formidable enemy and won, standing together against the odds.

With the Replicator threat finally eliminated, the universe was safe once more. The Doctor and his companions knew that there would always be new challenges and adventures ahead, but they were ready to face them together.

As the TARDIS dematerialized, the Doctor looked at his friends, his eyes filled with hope. "Onward, to new adventures."

Rose, standing beside him, smiled. "To the end, Doctor."

With their spirits high and their resolve unwavering, the team looked forward to the future, ready to protect the universe from any threat, standing united until the very end, never forgetting the heroes who had given everything for their victory.

Chapter 43: Replicator Downfall

The TARDIS materialized on the central battlefield, a place now scarred with the remnants of countless battles. The air was heavy with anticipation and tension. The combined forces of UNIT, Torchwood, SG-1, and the Doctor stood ready to deploy the final plan: activating the ancient weapon designed to seed life in the universe, now repurposed to eradicate the Replicators by targeting their electrical bonds.

The Doctor, standing at the TARDIS console, adjusted the controls with a mix of urgency and precision. Around him were Rose, Jack Harkness, Sarah Jane, and SG-1, each prepared for the roles they would play in this decisive moment. Kate Stewart's voice crackled through the comms, coordinating from UNIT headquarters.

"All units, this is it," Kate said, her voice firm and clear. "We need to activate the ancient weapon and find the right frequency to disrupt the Replicators' electrical bonds. Once we do, we'll initiate a synchronized energy blast to wipe them out."

Colonel O'Neill, checking his weapon, nodded. "Alright, people. This is our final push. Let's make it count."

Major Carter, her face set with determination, added, "We've integrated the ancient weapon with the TARDIS's systems. We need to find the precise frequency modulation to disrupt their bonds."

Teal'c, his expression stoic, said, "The Replicators will not fall without a fight. We must be prepared for their counterattack."

Jack Harkness, grinning confidently, adjusted his gear. "Let's give these Replicators a proper send-off."

Daniel Jackson, holding the ancient texts and translations, stepped forward. "Doctor, according to the texts, the weapon uses a fluctuating frequency to create an energy bubble. This bubble will expand and disrupt the Replicators at their core."

The Doctor nodded, his eyes fixed on the holographic display showing the locations of the remaining Replicator strongholds. "Alright, everyone. Take your positions. We need to find the right frequency and activate the weapon. Stay sharp and watch each other's backs."

The Search for the Frequency

The team moved quickly, setting up the ancient weapon in the heart of the battlefield. The TARDIS's central console glowed with energy as the Doctor and Major Carter calibrated the frequency modulation.

"We need to match the frequency of their electrical bonds," Carter explained, adjusting the controls. "If we get this wrong, the weapon won't work."

The Doctor, using his sonic screwdriver, scanned the Replicator remains for the precise frequency. "Almost there... we need to fine-tune it just a bit more."

Rose and Jack provided cover, their eyes scanning the horizon for any sign of Replicator reinforcements. "We've got your back, Doctor," Rose called out.

Sarah Jane, monitoring the power levels, added, "The weapon is charging. We're at 75% capacity."

As the Doctor and Carter worked, the Replicators launched a fierce counterattack. Swarms of metallic and organic bodies surged towards the team, their movements erratic and deadly.

"Engage!" O'Neill shouted, opening fire. "Hold them off until the weapon is ready!"

Teal'c, his staff weapon blazing, moved with precision, taking down Replicators with each shot. "We must protect the weapon at all costs."

Jack Harkness, firing relentlessly, grinned. "Let's give them hell!"

The Activation

With a final adjustment, the Doctor and Carter found the precise frequency. The ancient weapon began to hum with a powerful energy, its core glowing with a blinding light.

"We've got it!" Carter shouted. "The frequency is locked in!"

The Doctor activated the weapon, and a beam of pure, resonating energy shot out, enveloping the battlefield. The frequency modulation created a massive energy bubble, which began to expand rapidly.

"It's working!" Rose shouted, her voice filled with hope. "They're breaking apart!"

The Replicators convulsed violently, their forms disintegrating as the energy bubble spread through their ranks. The battlefield was filled with the sounds of their destruction, a chaotic symphony of victory.

"Keep the pressure on!" O'Neill commanded. "We're almost there!"

Teal'c, ever calm, added, "We must not relent."

The energy bubble continued to expand, engulfing the Replicator strongholds. The feedback loop created a cascading failure, spreading through their entire network.

The Final Battle

The Replicators, driven by desperation, launched a final, ferocious assault. Swarms of metallic and organic bodies surged towards the team, determined to stop the weapon.

"Hold the line!" O'Neill commanded. "We can't let them overwhelm us!"

Teal'c, his staff weapon blazing, provided cover fire. "We must maintain our position."

Jack Harkness, firing relentlessly, grinned. "We've got them on the ropes! Just a little more!"

As the energy bubble reached its peak, the Replicators' network began to collapse. Their forms disintegrated into dust, their electrical bonds shattered by the fluctuating frequency.

"We're nearing the end," Carter reported, monitoring the readings. "The Replicators' network is collapsing."

The Doctor, his eyes fixed on the viewscreen, saw the final stronghold disintegrate. "It's over. We've done it."

The Aftermath

The battlefield fell silent as the last of the Replicators disintegrated. The team, battered but triumphant, regrouped and began to make their way back to the TARDIS.

"We did it," Sarah Jane said, tears streaming down her face. "It's finally over."

Colonel O'Neill nodded, his face reflecting a mix of exhaustion and triumph. "Good job, everyone. We held the line."

Teal'c, ever stoic, added, "The Replicators are defeated. We have succeeded."

Jack Harkness grinned broadly. "That was one for the history books."

The Doctor, his hearts swelling with pride and gratitude, addressed his companions. "We faced impossible odds and emerged victorious. We did it together, as a team. The universe is safe because of all of you."

Rassilon's voice echoed through the comms, filled with respect. "You have done Gallifrey proud, Doctor. The Time Lords owe you and your allies a great debt."

Kate Stewart, her face reflecting the weariness of battle but also immense pride, nodded. "UNIT, Torchwood, SG-1, and the Doctor's team—together, we achieved the impossible."

As the team tended to the wounded and began to repair the damage, there was a sense of unity and triumph. They had faced a formidable enemy and won, standing together against the odds.

With the Replicator threat finally eliminated, the universe was safe once more. The Doctor and his companions knew that there would always be new challenges and adventures ahead, but they were ready to face them together.

As the TARDIS dematerialized, the Doctor looked at his friends, his eyes filled with hope. "Onward, to new adventures."

Rose, standing beside him, smiled. "To the end, Doctor."

With their spirits high and their resolve unwavering, the team looked forward to the future, ready to protect the universe from any threat, standing united until the very end, never forgetting the heroes who had given everything for their victory.

Chapter 44: Final Stand

The TARDIS rematerialized on the scorched battlefield, the air still crackling with residual energy from the ancient weapon's devastating blast. The combined forces of UNIT, Torchwood, and SG-1 began to regroup, their faces showing both relief and exhaustion. The energy weapon had eradicated the vast majority of the Replicators, but the heroes knew they needed to make one final sweep to ensure no remnants were left behind.

The Doctor stepped out of the TARDIS, his sonic screwdriver in hand. Rose, Jack Harkness, Sarah Jane, and SG-1 followed, each prepared for the final cleanup operation.

"Alright, everyone," the Doctor said, his voice steady but filled with urgency. "We've dealt a significant blow to the Replicators, but we need to ensure every last one is destroyed. Leave no stone unturned."

Colonel O'Neill, ever the pragmatist, checked his weapon. "You heard the man. Let's get to it."

Major Carter, her eyes sharp with determination, added, "We'll split into teams and sweep the area. Any remaining Replicators could regroup if we don't take them out."

Teal'c, his expression stoic, said, "We must be thorough. The Replicators are resourceful and will not give up easily."

Jack Harkness grinned confidently. "Let's mop up the stragglers."

Sarah Jane, scanning the area with her portable device, nodded. "I'm picking up faint signals. We've still got work to do."

The Sweep

The teams split into smaller units, each tasked with sweeping a designated sector of the battlefield. The air was thick with the smell of burnt metal and the faint hum of deactivated Replicators.

The Doctor led one team, with Rose and Jack by his side. They moved through the ruins, their eyes scanning for any sign of movement.

"Stay alert," the Doctor warned. "Even one Replicator can be dangerous."

Rose, her weapon at the ready, nodded. "I'm on it, Doctor."

Jack, ever the optimist, grinned. "We'll find them."

As they moved deeper into the ruins, a faint clicking sound caught their attention. The Doctor raised his sonic screwdriver, scanning the area.

"There," he said, pointing to a pile of debris. "Under the rubble."

Jack and Rose moved quickly, shifting the debris to reveal a damaged but still functional Replicator. It clicked and whirred, attempting to reassemble itself.

"Not today," Jack said, firing his weapon and destroying the Replicator.

Meanwhile, with SG-1 and UNIT

Colonel O'Neill and Teal'c led another team through the crumbling remains of a Replicator stronghold. Major Carter and Daniel Jackson scanned the area with their devices, searching for any remaining signals.

"I'm picking up something," Carter said, her voice tense. "There's a cluster of Replicators nearby."

O'Neill nodded. "Let's move."

The team advanced cautiously, their weapons ready. As they rounded a corner, they found a small group of Replicators attempting to rebuild a communications node.

"Engage!" O'Neill shouted, opening fire.

Teal'c, his staff weapon blazing, moved with precision, taking down Replicators with each shot. "We must destroy the node."

Daniel Jackson, using a portable energy device, targeted the communications node. "We need to disrupt their network completely."

Carter, providing cover fire, added, "Almost there!"

With a final blast, the node exploded, and the Replicators convulsed violently before disintegrating into dust.

The Final Push

As the teams continued their sweep, the residual Replicator signals grew weaker. The Doctor, using his sonic screwdriver, scanned the area for any remaining threats.

"We're almost done," he said, his voice filled with determination. "Just a few more."

Rose, her eyes sharp, spotted movement in the shadows. "There! Another one!"

Jack and the Doctor moved quickly, neutralizing the last Replicator with precise shots. The battlefield fell silent once more, the last remnants of the Replicators finally eradicated.

The Aftermath

The teams regrouped at the TARDIS, their faces showing a mix of exhaustion and triumph. The Replicator threat had been eliminated, thanks to their unwavering determination and teamwork.

"We did it," Sarah Jane said, tears of relief in her eyes. "It's finally over."

Colonel O'Neill nodded, his face reflecting a mix of exhaustion and triumph. "Good job, everyone. We held the line."

Teal'c, ever stoic, added, "The Replicators are defeated. We have succeeded."

Jack Harkness grinned broadly. "That was one for the history books."

The Doctor, his hearts swelling with pride and gratitude, addressed his companions. "We faced impossible odds and emerged victorious. We did it together, as a team. The universe is safe because of all of you."

Rassilon's voice echoed through the comms, filled with respect. "You have done Gallifrey proud, Doctor. The Time Lords owe you and your allies a great debt."

Kate Stewart, her face reflecting the weariness of battle but also immense pride, nodded. "UNIT, Torchwood, SG-1, and the Doctor's team—together, we achieved the impossible."

As the team tended to the wounded and began to repair the damage, there was a sense of unity and triumph. They had faced a formidable enemy and won, standing together against the odds.

With the Replicator threat finally eliminated, the universe was safe once more. The Doctor and his companions knew that there would always be new challenges and adventures ahead, but they were ready to face them together.

As the TARDIS dematerialized, the Doctor looked at his friends, his eyes filled with hope. "Onward, to new adventures."

Rose, standing beside him, smiled. "To the end, Doctor."

With their spirits high and their resolve unwavering, the team looked forward to the future, ready to protect the universe from any threat, standing united until the very end, never forgetting the heroes who had given everything for their victory.

Chapter 45: Victory Achieved

The TARDIS stood in the heart of the UNIT command center, a silent sentinel amid the remnants of a fierce battle. The air was heavy with the residual hum of advanced technology and the scent of scorched metal. For the first time in what felt like an eternity, there was a palpable sense of peace. The Replicators had been defeated, and the universe was finally free from their relentless threat.

The Doctor, his face etched with exhaustion but glowing with triumph, gathered his closest allies in the TARDIS control room. Rose, Jack Harkness, Sarah Jane, and the members of SG-1 stood around him, their expressions reflecting a mix of relief and disbelief. Kate Stewart and Rassilon joined via holographic link, their faces showing immense pride.

"We did it," the Doctor said, his voice resonating with a sense of awe and gratitude. "The Replicators are finally defeated. The universe can breathe a sigh of relief."

Rose, her eyes shining with tears, stepped forward and hugged the Doctor tightly. "We really did it, Doctor. It's finally over."

Jack Harkness, ever the optimist, grinned broadly. "I always knew we'd pull through. This team is unbeatable."

Sarah Jane, her voice choked with emotion, added, "So many sacrifices, but we made it. The universe is safe again."

Colonel O'Neill, standing with his arms crossed, nodded. "Good job, everyone. We held the line and came out on top."

Major Carter, her face reflecting a mix of exhaustion and triumph, said, "We couldn't have done it without each and every one of you. This victory belongs to us all."

Teal'c, ever the stoic warrior, added, "The Replicators have been eradicated. The universe owes us a great debt."

Daniel Jackson, his eyes filled with relief, said, "The Ancients' technology, the Asgard's help, and the Time Lords' guidance—we couldn't have asked for a better alliance."

Rassilon's holographic image nodded with respect. "You have done Gallifrey proud, Doctor. The Time Lords owe you and your allies a great debt."

Kate Stewart, her face reflecting the weariness of battle but also immense pride, nodded. "UNIT, Torchwood, SG-1, and the Doctor's team—together, we achieved the impossible."

The Aftermath

The team began to dismantle the temporary command center, their movements slow but filled with a sense of accomplishment. The battlefield, once a place of chaos and destruction, was now silent and still. The last remnants of the Replicators had been cleared, and the universe was finally free from their terror.

The Doctor, standing at the TARDIS console, looked at his friends with immense pride. "This victory is because of all of you. We faced impossible odds and emerged victorious. The universe is safe because of your courage and determination."

Rose, standing beside him, smiled through her tears. "We couldn't have done it without you, Doctor. You gave us hope when we needed it most."

Jack Harkness, always ready with a quip, added, "And a few good plans didn't hurt either."

Sarah Jane, her voice filled with warmth, said, "We're a team, Doctor. We always have been, and we always will be."

Colonel O'Neill, ever the leader, nodded. "We held the line together. That's what makes us strong."

Major Carter, her face showing both relief and pride, added, "We've proven that when we stand united, nothing can stop us."

Teal'c, his expression solemn, said, "The bonds forged in this battle will endure. We have become stronger because of it."

Daniel Jackson, his voice filled with gratitude, said, "We've made history here today. The universe will remember this victory."

Rassilon's holographic image shimmered with approval. "The Time Lords will honor your bravery and sacrifice. The universe owes you a debt that can never be repaid."

Kate Stewart, her face glowing with pride, nodded. "UNIT, Torchwood, SG-1, and the Doctor's team—together, we have shown the true meaning of unity and courage."

A Time to Reflect

As the TARDIS dematerialized from the battlefield and reappeared in a peaceful meadow on Earth, the team took a moment to reflect on their journey. The sun was setting, casting a warm golden light over the landscape. It was a stark contrast to the chaos and destruction they had faced, a symbol of the peace they had fought so hard to achieve.

The Doctor, standing at the TARDIS door, looked out over the serene landscape. "This is what we fight for," he said softly. "For moments like this, where the universe can be at peace."

Rose, standing beside him, nodded. "It's beautiful, Doctor. We did good."

Jack Harkness, grinning, added, "And we'll be ready for the next challenge, whatever it may be."

Sarah Jane, her eyes filled with warmth, said, "We've come a long way, and we'll go even further."

Colonel O'Neill, his face showing a rare moment of vulnerability, nodded. "We're a family now. And families stick together."

Major Carter, her eyes shining with determination, added, "We'll face whatever comes next, together."

Teal'c, ever the warrior, said, "We are stronger because of this. We will endure."

Daniel Jackson, his voice filled with conviction, said, "The universe is a better place because of what we've done."

Rassilon's voice echoed in their minds, filled with respect. "The Time Lords will always stand by you. You have our eternal gratitude."

Kate Stewart, her face reflecting pride and hope, nodded. "UNIT, Torchwood, SG-1, and the Doctor's team—together, we will face whatever the future holds."

As the sun dipped below the horizon, the team stood together, united by their shared victory and their unwavering determination. The universe was safe once more, but they knew that their journey was far from over. There would always be new challenges and new adventures, but they were ready to face them together, standing united until the very end.

With the TARDIS at their side and their spirits high, the team looked forward to the future, ready to protect the universe from any threat, never forgetting the heroes who had given everything for their victory.

Chapter 46: Aftermath

The TARDIS had transported the combined forces of UNIT, Torchwood, and SG-1 back to Earth. The battle against the Replicators was finally over, but the impact of their struggle lingered heavily in the air. The sky was a soft gradient of oranges and purples as the sun began to set, casting a serene light over the meadow where the teams had gathered to reflect on their victory and mourn their losses.

The Doctor stood near the TARDIS, watching the horizon. His face, usually so animated, was now marked with a contemplative expression. Rose approached him, her eyes filled with empathy.

"Doctor," Rose said softly, "We did it. We saved the universe."

The Doctor nodded, his gaze still fixed on the distance. "Yes, Rose. We did. But victory always comes at a cost."

Nearby, Jack Harkness was sharing a laugh with Colonel O'Neill, their bond forged in the fires of battle now solidified in camaraderie. Major Carter and Daniel Jackson were discussing the integration of ancient and modern technologies that had been pivotal in their success, their minds already at work on the implications of their discoveries.

Sarah Jane, standing with Teal'c, watched the interaction between the teams. "It's incredible, isn't it? How we all came together."

Teal'c nodded solemnly. "Indeed. Unity in the face of adversity has proven to be our greatest strength."

Kate Stewart, overseeing the disbanding of the temporary command center, joined the group. "We've achieved the impossible. But now, we have to deal with the aftermath."

Mourning the Fallen

A makeshift memorial had been set up in the meadow, a quiet space where the heroes could pay their respects to those who had fallen. Pictures of Jack Harkness, Major Carter, and other brave souls who had sacrificed everything adorned the memorial, surrounded by candles flickering in the gentle breeze.

The Doctor approached the memorial, his hearts heavy with the weight of the lives lost. He placed a hand on a photograph of Jack Harkness, his voice barely above a whisper. "You always said you'd fight to the end, Jack. And you did."

Rose stood beside him, tears streaming down her face. "They were all so brave. They gave everything."

Colonel O'Neill and Teal'c joined them, their faces etched with solemn respect. "Carter... she would have been proud of what we accomplished," O'Neill said, his voice rough with emotion.

Teal'c bowed his head. "Their sacrifices will not be forgotten. They live on in our victory."

Sarah Jane, her eyes filled with tears, placed a flower at the memorial. "We'll remember them. Always."

Celebrating the Victory

As night fell, the mood in the meadow shifted from solemn remembrance to quiet celebration. A bonfire crackled, providing warmth and light. The teams shared stories of their fallen comrades, laughing and crying together as they honored their memories.

Jack Harkness, his usual boisterous self, was sorely missed. But his spirit seemed to linger in the jokes and anecdotes shared around the fire.

"Remember that time Jack tried to flirt his way out of a Dalek extermination?" Rose said, a smile breaking through her tears.

O'Neill chuckled. "Classic Harkness. The man had guts, that's for sure."

Major Carter's contributions were also fondly remembered, her brilliance and bravery celebrated by all who had fought alongside her.

"She always had the answer, didn't she?" Daniel Jackson said, his voice filled with admiration. "No problem was too big for her."

The Doctor, feeling a surge of pride for his friends, spoke up. "We faced one of the greatest threats the universe has ever known, and we stood together. We honored our fallen by achieving the impossible. Their legacy is our victory."

Kate Stewart raised a toast, her voice carrying a note of resolve. "To the heroes who gave everything, and to the future we've secured. We will continue to protect the universe in their honor."

Looking to the Future

As the night grew darker, the teams began to disperse, each group returning to their respective organizations with a renewed sense of purpose and unity.

The Doctor, Rose, Sarah Jane, and the members of SG-1 stood together for a final moment of reflection.

"What now, Doctor?" Rose asked, her eyes filled with curiosity and hope.

The Doctor smiled, a twinkle of adventure returning to his eyes. "Now, we move forward. There will always be new challenges, new adventures. But we face them together, as a family."

Colonel O'Neill extended his hand. "It's been an honor, Doctor. If you ever need us again, you know where to find us."

Teal'c nodded. "We shall remain vigilant. The universe is vast, and there is always more to learn."

Sarah Jane hugged the Doctor tightly. "Stay safe, Doctor. And remember, you're never alone."

The Doctor, his hearts swelling with gratitude and love for his friends, nodded. "None of us are."

As the TARDIS doors closed and the familiar sound of dematerialization filled the air, the Doctor and his companions set off for new adventures, their spirits high and their resolve unwavering.

Epilogue: A Universe at Peace

The universe, for the first time in what felt like eons, was at peace. The Replicator threat had been eradicated, and the heroes who had fought so valiantly could finally rest. Their sacrifices had not been in vain; they had secured a future free from the terror of the Replicators.

The stars shone brightly in the night sky, a testament to the bravery and unity of those who had fought to protect the universe. The legacy of the heroes would live on, inspiring future generations to stand together in the face of adversity.

As the TARDIS traveled through the cosmos, the Doctor looked out at the endless expanse of stars. "Onward, to new adventures," he whispered, a smile playing at his lips.

Rose, standing beside him, nodded. "To the end, Doctor."

And so, the journey continued, with the Doctor and his companions ready to face whatever challenges lay ahead, united in their mission to protect the universe and honor the memory of the heroes who had given everything for their victory.

Chapter 47: Restoration

The TARDIS materialized in the heart of what was once a bustling city, now left in ruins after the fierce battles against the Replicators. The air was filled with the sound of machinery and construction as efforts to restore the damaged parts of Earth and Gallifrey began in earnest. The combined forces of UNIT, Torchwood, SG-1, and the Time Lords worked tirelessly, sharing their advanced technologies to ensure a lasting peace between worlds and the rest of the universe.

The Doctor, Rose, Jack Harkness, Sarah Jane, and the members of SG-1 stepped out of the TARDIS, their faces set with determination and hope. They were greeted by Kate Stewart, Rassilon, and a team of engineers and scientists from across Earth and Gallifrey.

"Welcome, Doctor," Kate said, her voice filled with a mix of relief and determination. "We've made significant progress, but there's still a lot of work to be done."

Rassilon, his presence imposing yet filled with respect, nodded. "The Time Lords are committed to aiding in the restoration. Our combined knowledge will ensure that this world, and Gallifrey, are stronger than ever."

The Doctor smiled, his eyes twinkling with a sense of purpose. "Together, we'll rebuild. We'll make sure that the sacrifices made were not in vain."

Restoration Efforts Begin

The combined teams set to work, their efforts a testament to the unity forged in the fires of battle. Advanced technologies from the Asgard, Time Lords, and Ancients were integrated into the rebuilding process, creating a foundation for a brighter future.

Major Carter, overseeing the integration of Asgard technology, addressed the gathered engineers. "We'll be using Asgard energy modulation to stabilize the power grid. This will ensure a sustainable and resilient energy source for the cities."

Daniel Jackson, working with a team of archaeologists and engineers, added, "The Ancients' knowledge will help us reconstruct the infrastructure, making it more efficient and advanced."

Teal'c, assisting with the construction efforts, said, "We must ensure that the new structures are not only strong but also capable of withstanding any future threats."

Jack Harkness, coordinating the efforts of Torchwood, grinned. "And we'll be making sure that our defenses are top-notch. No more surprises."

Earth's Restoration

In cities across Earth, the combined forces worked tirelessly. Skyscrapers that had been reduced to rubble were rebuilt using a combination of human ingenuity and advanced alien technology. The streets, once filled with debris, were now bustling with activity as people worked together to restore their homes.

Sarah Jane, overseeing a group of volunteers, smiled as she watched the progress. "It's amazing what we can achieve when we work together."

Rose, helping to distribute supplies, nodded. "We're building a better future, one brick at a time."

The Doctor, moving from site to site, provided guidance and encouragement. "Remember, this isn't just about rebuilding what was lost. It's about creating something new, something better."

Gallifrey's Restoration

On Gallifrey, the Time Lords worked alongside their newfound allies to restore their once-majestic cities. The golden spires of the Citadel, damaged in the conflict, were repaired using a blend of Time Lord and Asgard technology, ensuring their resilience for millennia to come.

Rassilon, overseeing the restoration, addressed the gathered Time Lords and engineers. "Our world has endured great trials, but we will emerge stronger. Our alliance with Earth and the other worlds will ensure that Gallifrey stands as a beacon of hope and knowledge."

The Doctor, visiting Gallifrey, looked around with a sense of pride. "We've faced so much, but look at what we're achieving. Together, we're unstoppable."

Advancements in Technology

The integration of Asgard, Time Lord, and Ancient technologies led to remarkable advancements. Medical facilities were equipped with advanced healing technologies, ensuring that injuries and illnesses could be treated swiftly and effectively. Energy grids powered by Asgard technology provided sustainable and virtually limitless power.

Major Carter, demonstrating the new energy systems, explained, "This technology not only stabilizes the power grid but also ensures that we're not dependent on limited resources. It's a game-changer."

Daniel Jackson, working on the integration of Ancient knowledge, added, "The Ancients' understanding of physics and engineering will allow us to build infrastructure that's not only advanced but also adaptable to future needs."

The Doctor, overseeing the advancements, smiled. "We're creating a foundation for a future where technology and humanity work hand in hand. A future where knowledge and compassion lead the way."

Ensuring Lasting Peace

As the restoration efforts continued, the focus also turned to ensuring lasting peace between the worlds. Diplomatic relations were strengthened, and alliances were formalized to ensure that the unity forged in battle would endure in times of peace.

Kate Stewart, addressing a gathering of diplomats and leaders, said, "The battle against the Replicators showed us what we can achieve when we stand together. Now, we must ensure that this unity continues, fostering cooperation and mutual respect."

Rassilon, representing the Time Lords, added, "Gallifrey stands ready to support our allies in any way possible. Together, we will ensure that peace and knowledge prevail."

The Doctor, his hearts swelling with pride, addressed the gathered leaders. "We've faced the darkest of times and emerged victorious. Now, let's build a future where such darkness can never take root again. A future of peace, understanding, and endless possibility."

A New Dawn

As the sun rose over the restored cities of Earth and Gallifrey, there was a sense of renewal and hope. The combined efforts of the heroes had not only rebuilt what was lost but also laid the groundwork for a brighter future.

The Doctor, standing with Rose, Jack, Sarah Jane, and SG-1, looked out over the horizon. "This is just the beginning. The universe is vast and filled with wonders. And we'll face whatever comes next, together."

Rose, her eyes filled with determination, nodded. "To new adventures, Doctor."

Jack Harkness, grinning broadly, added, "And to a future we can all be proud of."

Sarah Jane, her voice filled with warmth, said, "We've come so far, and we'll go even further."

Colonel O'Neill, Major Carter, Teal'c, and Daniel Jackson stood with them, their faces reflecting a shared sense of accomplishment and hope.

As the TARDIS dematerialized, the Doctor looked at his friends, his eyes filled with hope. "Onward, to new adventures."

With their spirits high and their resolve unwavering, the team looked forward to the future, ready to protect the universe from any threat, standing united until the very end, never forgetting the heroes who had given everything for their victory and the bright future they had secured.

Chapter 48: Farewells

The TARDIS stood on the edge of a tranquil meadow, a place where the combined forces of UNIT, Torchwood, SG-1, and the Doctor had gathered for one final time before parting ways. The sun was setting, casting a golden glow over the landscape, and there was a sense of both closure and new beginnings in the air.

The Doctor, standing at the TARDIS door, looked out at the assembled friends and allies, his hearts heavy with the impending farewells. Beside him were Rose, Jack Harkness, Sarah Jane, and the members of SG-1, each ready to embark on their next journey.

Farewell to SG-1

Colonel O'Neill, Major Carter, Teal'c, and Daniel Jackson approached the Doctor, their faces reflecting a mix of gratitude and respect.

"Doctor," O'Neill began, his voice steady, "It's been an honor working with you. We've faced impossible odds and come out on top. Thanks to you, we've seen things we never thought possible."

The Doctor smiled warmly. "The honor has been mine, Colonel. You and your team are some of the bravest people I've ever met. The universe is a safer place because of you."

Carter stepped forward, her eyes filled with admiration. "Doctor, your knowledge and courage have been inspiring. We've learned so much from you."

The Doctor nodded. "And I from you, Major Carter. Your brilliance and dedication are unparalleled. Keep pushing the boundaries of what's possible."

Teal'c bowed slightly, his expression solemn. "Doctor, you have shown us the power of unity and compassion. You will always have allies in the Jaffa."

"Thank you, Teal'c," the Doctor replied. "Your strength and honor have been invaluable. May our paths cross again in peace."

Daniel Jackson, holding a small ancient artifact as a token of remembrance, handed it to the Doctor. "Doctor, you've opened our eyes to the wonders of the universe. This is a small token of our appreciation."

The Doctor accepted the artifact with a nod. "Thank you, Daniel. Your curiosity and wisdom are what drive us forward. Never stop seeking the truth."

Farewell to Torchwood

Jack Harkness, his usual grin softened by the moment, stepped forward with his Torchwood team.

"Doctor," Jack began, his voice carrying a note of emotion, "It's been one hell of a ride. You've saved the universe more times than I can count, and it's been an honor to fight by your side."

The Doctor clasped Jack's hand firmly. "Jack, you've been a constant friend and ally. Torchwood is in good hands with you. Keep fighting the good fight."

Jack nodded, his eyes shining. "You can count on it, Doctor. And if you ever need us, just call."

Gwen Cooper, standing beside Jack, added, "Thank you, Doctor. You've shown us that there's always hope, even in the darkest times."

The Doctor smiled warmly. "Gwen, your courage and compassion are what make Torchwood great. Keep looking after each other."

Farewell to UNIT

Kate Stewart and her UNIT team approached next, their faces reflecting pride and gratitude.

"Doctor," Kate began, her voice steady, "UNIT owes you a great debt. You've been our guide and protector, and we're stronger because of you."

The Doctor nodded. "Kate, UNIT's dedication to protecting the Earth is unwavering. Keep up the good work, and never stop believing in the impossible."

Kate smiled. "We won't, Doctor. And we'll always be here to help."

Farewell to Sarah Jane

Sarah Jane Smith, her eyes filled with warmth, stepped forward. "Doctor, it's been a journey I'll never forget. You've shown me the wonders of the universe and the power of friendship."

The Doctor took her hands in his. "Sarah Jane, you've always been more than just a companion. You're family. Your bravery and heart have saved countless lives. Keep shining your light."

Sarah Jane nodded, tears in her eyes. "I will, Doctor. And I'll never forget you."

Farewell to Rose

Finally, it was time to say goodbye to Rose Tyler. The bond between her and the Doctor was deep, forged through countless adventures and shared moments of triumph and heartache.

"Doctor," Rose began, her voice trembling slightly, "I don't know how to say goodbye. You've changed my life in ways I can't even begin to describe."

The Doctor's eyes were filled with emotion. "Rose, you've been my strength, my heart. You've shown me the beauty of humanity. This isn't goodbye. Not really."

Rose nodded, tears streaming down her face. "I know. I'll always carry you with me, wherever I go."

The Doctor pulled her into a tight embrace, holding her close. "And I'll always be with you, Rose. In every star, in every sky."

As they parted, the Doctor looked at the assembled friends and allies, his hearts swelling with pride and gratitude.

"We've faced impossible odds and emerged victorious," he said, his voice carrying a note of finality. "But this is just the beginning. The universe is vast and filled with wonders. Our paths may diverge, but we'll always be united by the bonds we've forged."

With final hugs and handshakes, the teams began to disperse, each group returning to their respective organizations with a renewed sense of purpose and unity.

A New Dawn

As the TARDIS dematerialized, the Doctor looked at his friends one last time, his eyes filled with hope. "Onward, to new adventures."

Rose, standing beside him, smiled through her tears. "To the end, Doctor."

With their spirits high and their resolve unwavering, the Doctor and his companions set off for new adventures, ready to protect the universe from any threat, standing united until the very end, never forgetting the heroes who had given everything for their victory and the bright future they had secured.

Chapter 49: New Beginnings

The TARDIS hummed with a renewed sense of purpose as it traveled through the vortex, carrying the Doctor and Sarah Jane Smith toward their next adventure. The console room was filled with the familiar glow of the central column, casting a warm light over the duo as they prepared to embark on a journey that symbolized both new beginnings and a tribute to their shared past.

The Doctor, his usual energy tempered with reflection, adjusted the controls with a deft touch. Beside him, Sarah Jane looked around with a mix of nostalgia and excitement. She had been away from the TARDIS for a while, but stepping back inside felt like coming home.

"Where to this time, Doctor?" Sarah Jane asked, her eyes sparkling with anticipation.

The Doctor grinned, the spark of adventure returning to his eyes. "The universe is our oyster, Sarah Jane. How about we visit the Helix Nebula? It's known as the Eye of God, quite a sight to behold."

Sarah Jane chuckled. "Always the poet, Doctor. The Helix Nebula it is."

The Journey Begins

As the TARDIS dematerialized and reappeared near the Helix Nebula, the viewscreen displayed a breathtaking sight: a vast, swirling cloud of gas and dust, glowing in shades of blue and red, with a brilliant white core at its center.

"Wow," Sarah Jane whispered, her eyes wide with wonder. "It's beautiful."

The Doctor nodded, his gaze fixed on the nebula. "It's moments like these that remind us why we do what we do. The universe is full of beauty, even in the midst of chaos."

They stood in silence for a moment, absorbing the beauty of the nebula. It was a peaceful interlude, a stark contrast to the battles they had recently fought.

A New Mystery

Their moment of tranquility was interrupted by a series of beeps and blips from the console. The Doctor frowned and began to scan the data.

"Doctor, what is it?" Sarah Jane asked, sensing his shift in focus.

The Doctor's expression grew serious. "I'm picking up a distress signal. It's coming from a nearby planet, Veloria Prime. It's a cry for help."

Sarah Jane's face mirrored his concern. "We have to help them, Doctor. We can't ignore a distress signal."

The Doctor nodded. "Absolutely. Veloria Prime, here we come."

The TARDIS materialized on the surface of Veloria Prime, a lush, verdant planet with towering trees and a vibrant ecosystem. The distress signal led them to a small village, where the inhabitants were gathered in a state of panic.

A village elder, a tall figure with silvery hair and wise eyes, approached the Doctor and Sarah Jane. "Thank the stars you've come. We need your help."

The Doctor stepped forward, his voice filled with reassurance. "We received your distress signal. What's happening here?"

The elder, named Liora, explained, "Our village has been under attack by mysterious creatures. They come at night, taking our people and leaving destruction in their wake."

Sarah Jane, always empathetic, asked, "Have you seen these creatures? Do you know what they are?"

Liora shook her head. "They move too quickly, and they blend into the shadows. We're helpless against them."

The Doctor's mind raced with possibilities. "We'll help you. We need to set up a perimeter and gather more information about these creatures."

The Investigation

The Doctor and Sarah Jane spent the day setting up scanners and preparing the village for the night. As darkness fell, they kept watch, waiting for the creatures to appear.

Suddenly, a series of loud crashes and terrified screams echoed through the village. The Doctor and Sarah Jane sprang into action, their eyes scanning the darkness for any sign of movement.

"There!" Sarah Jane shouted, pointing to a shadowy figure darting between the trees.

The Doctor used his sonic screwdriver to illuminate the area, revealing a sleek, black creature with glowing red eyes. The creature hissed and lunged at them, but the Doctor quickly adjusted the sonic screwdriver, emitting a high-pitched frequency that repelled the creature.

The Doctor and Sarah Jane chased the creature through the village, eventually cornering it near the edge of the forest. The creature, realizing it was trapped, emitted a series of clicks and chirps.

"Doctor, what's it saying?" Sarah Jane asked, her eyes wide with curiosity.

The Doctor listened intently. "It's communicating. It's not attacking out of malice; it's scared."

He approached the creature slowly, speaking in soothing tones. "We're not here to harm you. We want to help."

The creature, sensing the Doctor's sincerity, calmed down and allowed him to scan it with the sonic screwdriver. The data revealed that the creature was a member of a species called the Nyxari, displaced from their homeworld by an environmental catastrophe.

"The Nyxari were driven from their planet and are trying to survive here," the Doctor explained to the villagers. "They're not evil; they're desperate."

Liora, the village elder, listened with empathy. "What can we do to help them?"

A New Alliance

The Doctor proposed a plan to integrate the Nyxari into the village, providing them with the resources they needed to survive without causing harm. The villagers, guided by Liora's wisdom, agreed to the plan.

Over the next few days, the Doctor and Sarah Jane worked tirelessly to mediate between the villagers and the Nyxari. They built shelters, shared food, and taught the villagers how to communicate with the Nyxari.

One evening, as the sun set over the peaceful village, Liora approached the Doctor and Sarah Jane. "Thank you for bringing us together. We've learned that understanding and compassion can overcome fear."

Sarah Jane smiled warmly. "It's all about seeing the world through each other's eyes."

The Doctor nodded, his hearts filled with pride. "This is what it means to be a part of the universe. To help, to understand, and to grow together."

A New Beginning

With the crisis resolved and the villagers and Nyxari living in harmony, it was time for the Doctor and Sarah Jane to move on. They stood at the edge of the village, bidding farewell to their new friends.

"Thank you, Doctor," Liora said, her eyes shining with gratitude. "You've given us a new beginning."

The Doctor smiled. "The real thanks goes to you, Liora. You opened your hearts and minds to a new way of life."

Sarah Jane hugged Liora tightly. "Take care of each other. You're stronger together."

As the Doctor and Sarah Jane stepped back into the TARDIS, the familiar sound of dematerialization filled the air. They watched the village disappear from the viewscreen, their hearts light with the knowledge that they had made a difference.

"Where to next, Doctor?" Sarah Jane asked, her eyes sparkling with anticipation.

The Doctor grinned, his spirit of adventure reignited. "The universe is vast, Sarah Jane. Let's see what wonders await us."

And so, the TARDIS soared through the cosmos, carrying the Doctor and Sarah Jane toward new adventures, leaving behind a legacy of hope and unity, forever changed by their experiences but ready to face whatever challenges lay ahead with courage and compassion.

Chapter 50: Reflection

The TARDIS floated in the serene expanse of space, the stars twinkling like distant memories against the velvet darkness. Inside the console room, a gentle hum filled the air, mingling with the soft, rhythmic pulse of the central column. The Doctor stood alone at the console, his hands resting on the controls, his mind a whirlwind of thoughts and emotions.

Sarah Jane had taken a moment to rest in her quarters, leaving the Doctor to his solitude. The events of the recent battle against the Replicators and the aftermath were fresh in his mind, and he felt the weight of the sacrifices made pressing down on him.

The Doctor's gaze drifted to a small table nearby, where a collection of mementos lay. A photograph of Jack Harkness, Major Carter's insignia, a piece of ancient technology given to him by Daniel Jackson, and a small flower from Sarah Jane's makeshift memorial. Each item held a story, a reminder of the bravery and resilience of those who had fought alongside him.

With a heavy sigh, the Doctor activated the TARDIS's voice interface. The holographic image of a familiar face appeared before him, that of his previous companion, Clara Oswald.

"Hello, Doctor," the interface said, its voice gentle and understanding.

"Hello, Clara," the Doctor replied, his voice tinged with melancholy. "I needed someone to talk to."

The interface nodded. "You've been through a lot. It's only natural to feel the weight of it all."

The Doctor walked slowly around the console, his thoughts drifting back to the battle. "We faced impossible odds, Clara. So many brave souls gave everything to protect the universe. Jack, Major Carter, countless others. Their sacrifices were not in vain, but it's hard not to feel the loss."

The interface watched him with empathetic eyes. "They knew the risks, Doctor. They chose to fight because they believed in the cause. And they believed in you."

The Doctor paused, looking out at the stars through the TARDIS's viewscreen. "I've lived for so long, seen so much. But every loss feels like a new wound. I can't help but wonder if there was more I could have done."

The interface stepped closer, its gaze unwavering. "You've always done everything in your power to protect the innocent, to fight for what's right. That's what makes you the Doctor."

He nodded slowly, a small, sad smile forming on his lips. "Perhaps. But it doesn't make the pain any less real."

The interface reached out as if to touch his shoulder, its holographic hand passing through him. "The pain reminds you that you care, that you're still fighting for those who can't. It's what makes you who you are."

The Doctor took a deep breath, feeling a sense of resolve settling over him. "You're right. I can't change the past, but I can honor their memories by continuing to fight for the future."

The interface smiled. "That's the Doctor I know. Always moving forward, always protecting the universe."

Just then, Sarah Jane entered the console room, her presence a comforting reminder of the friendships that sustained him. "Doctor, everything alright?"

The Doctor turned to her, his smile growing warmer. "Yes, Sarah Jane. Just reflecting on everything that's happened."

She nodded, understanding his need to process the events. "We've been through a lot, haven't we? But we've also accomplished so much."

He walked over to her, his hearts filled with gratitude. "We have. And it's because of brave souls like you, Sarah Jane. I couldn't have done it without you."

Sarah Jane smiled, her eyes shining with kindness. "We're a team, Doctor. Always."

The Doctor turned back to the TARDIS console, a renewed sense of purpose in his eyes. "There's still so much to do, so many threats to face. But we'll face them together."

Sarah Jane placed a reassuring hand on his arm. "And we'll honor those we've lost by protecting the universe they fought for."

The Doctor nodded, his resolve unshakeable. "I vow to protect the universe from future threats, to stand against the darkness, no matter the cost. For Jack, for Major Carter, for all the brave souls who have sacrificed everything."

He looked out at the stars, his gaze filled with determination. "Onward, to new adventures. We'll face whatever comes next, united and strong."

As the TARDIS sailed through the cosmos, the Doctor and Sarah Jane stood side by side, ready to embrace the future and honor the past. The journey continued, filled with hope, courage, and

Message from the Author:

I hope you enjoyed this book, I love astrology and knew there was not a book such as this out on the shelf. I love metaphysical items as well. Please check out my other books:

-Life of Government Benefits

-My life of Hell

-My life with Hydrocephalus

-Red Sky

-World Domination:Woman's rule

-World Domination:Woman's Rule 2: The War

-Life and Banishment of Apophis: book 1

-The Kidney Friendly Diet

-The Ultimate Hemp Cookbook

-Creating a Dispensary(legally)

-Cleanliness throughout life: the importance of showering from childhood to adulthood.

-Strong Roots: The Risks of Overcoddling children

-Hemp Horoscopes: Cosmic Insights and Earthly Healing

- Celestial Hemp Navigating the Zodiac: Through the Green Cosmos

-Astrological Hemp: Aligning The Stars with Earth's Ancient Herb

-The Astrological Guide to Hemp: Stars, Signs, and Sacred Leaves

-Green Growth: Innovative Marketing Strategies for your Hemp Products and Dispensary

-Cosmic Cannabis

-Astrological Munchies

-Henry The Hemp

-Zodiacal Roots: The Astrological Soul Of Hemp

- **Green Constellations: Intersection of Hemp and Zodiac**

-Hemp in The Houses: An astrological Adventure Through The Cannabis Galaxy

-Galactic Ganja Guide

Heavenly Hemp

Zodiac Leaves

Doctor Who Astrology

Cannastrology

Stellar Satvias and Cosmic Indicas

Celestial Cannabis: A Zodiac Journey

AstroHerbology: The Sky and The Soil: Volume 1

AstroHerbology:Celestial Cannabis:Volume 2

Cosmic Cannabis Cultivation

The Starry Guide to Herbal Harmony: Volume 1

The Starry Guide to Herbal Harmony: Cannabis Universe: Volume 2

Yugioh Astrology: Astrological Guide to Deck, Duels and more

Nightmare Mansion: Echoes of The Abyss

Nightmare Mansion 2: Legacy of Shadows

Nightmare Mansion 3: Shadows of the Forgotten

Nightmare Mansion 4: Echoes of the Damned

The Life and Banishment of Apophis: Book 2

Nightmare Mansion: Halls of Despair

Healing with Herb: Cannabis and Hydrocephalus

Planetary Pot: Aligning with Astrological Herbs: Volume 1

Fast Track to Freedom: 30 Days to Financial Independence Using AI, Assets, and Agile Hustles

Cosmic Hemp Pathways

How to Become Financially Free in 30 Days: 10,000 Paths to Prosperity

Zodiacal Herbage: Astrological Insights: Volume 1

Nightmare Mansion: Whispers in the Walls

The Daleks Invade Atlantis

Henry the hemp and Hydrocephalus

10X The Kidney Friendly Diet

Cannabis Universe: Adult coloring book

Hemp Astrology: The Healing Power of the Stars

Zodiacal Herbage: Astrological Insights: Cannabis Universe: Volume 2

Planetary Pot: Aligning with Astrological Herbs: Cannabis Universes: Volume 2

Check out my Virtual dispensary for all your hemp needs: https://shift.store/sg1fan23477/retail

If you want solar for your home go here: https://www.harborsolar.live/apophisenterprises/

Get some shirts: https://www.bonfire.com/store/apophis-shirt-emporium/

Instagrams:

@apophis_enterprises,

@hempkingdom2024,

@apophisbookemporium,

@apophisfashion,

@apophisscardshop

Twitter: @apophisenterpr1,

Tiktok:@apophisenterprise

Youtube: @sg1fan23477

Podcast: Apophis Chat Zone: https://open.spotify.com/show/5zXbrCLEV2xzCp8ybrfHsk?si=fb4d4fdbdce44dec

Newsletter: https://apophiss-newsletter-27c897.beehiiv.com/

Coming Soon!
Sacred Serpent Tarot book and card set.

Sacred Serpents Tarot Card Example

| 225 |